THE IDEAL

L.P. Maxa

ALSO BY L.P. MAXA

RiffRaff Records

Royalty

Legacy

Infamy

Loyalty

Sanctuary

Piracy

Certainty

Inevitably

Finally

The Devil's Share

Play Nice

Play Dirty

Play Fair

Play Softly

Play Hard

Play For Keeps

St. Leasing

Mouth Watering

Breath Taking

Jaw Dropping

Heart Stopping

Soul Crushing

Other Novels

Happy Place

Stumbled into Love

Rescued

The Forever Weekend

www.BOROUGHSPUBLISHINGGROUP.com

THE IDEAL
Copyright © 2020 L.P. Maxa

ISBN: 978-1-953810-21-2

To anyone, everyone, who has ever gotten lost in love

ACKNOWLEDGMENTS

I started writing this book years ago, and it was a story I'd work on when I had the time, or when I needed a break from current projects. These characters were born in the real world, morphed and reworked in my mind, but without my editor, I wouldn't have put them out there for the world to meet. So this time, my first thank you is to Michelle. Thanks for believing in me, no matter what.

Thank you to my husband, who had two kiddos to watch this time around while I locked myself away to write. We adopted a beautiful baby girl, and we are so in love with our new family of four.

Thank you to all my readers for supporting me while I was on maternity leave, for being happy for me, and for coming with me on this journey. I will never take for granted how blessed I am to have all my dreams come true.

AUTHOR'S NOTE

Trigger Warning For People With Sensitivities To Certain Topics

While there are <u>no explicit scenes</u> depicting rape, there is one scene where it's attempted.

THE IDEAL

"She had not known the weight until she felt the freedom."
~Nathanial Hawthorne

Prologue

I grabbed Nathan's hands, desperately trying to pry them from around my throat. I could feel myself start to lose consciousness: the edges of my vison beginning to blur. I kicked and bucked, doing everything I could to get him off me. As I stared into his eyes—deep brown eyes that had once been so familiar and had now gone black—I knew Savy's secret was out.

The secret she and I had kept between us.

It had only ever been me for her.

Chapter One

Jeremy

I leaned back in my mesh lounge chair, closed my eyes and listened to the sound of Savy's laughter. I could picture her clear as day in my mind. Her head thrown back, and her beautiful slender neck washed in sunlight. I smiled when I heard my brother chuckle at whatever she was saying.

Savy was pretty much the only person who could make my brother happy. Make him let loose and have fun. Nathan was two years younger than me, and he and I were as different as night and day. We were raised in a cheerful home with loving, attentive parents. Where I aimed to please, treasured life, and went with the flow, Nathan bucked every request, directive, or order given to him. Since he was a baby, he was stubborn and dark. We were the perfect example of nature versus nurture. A psychologist's wet dream.

Our dad had always been able to keep Nathan in line. Keep him from throwing epic fits and hurting innocent people in the process. But Dad had been gone for eight years now. A simple mistake had taken him from us too soon. His sudden death had us all reeling.

Nathan without my father was a loaded gun begging to be picked up and played with. The responsibility of being Nathan's keeper should've fallen to my mom, or even to me. But it'd gone to the girl next door, Savannah Nightingale. She was light to Nathan's dark. She brought him back into the land of the living time and time again. She kept him human.

When Nathan was thirteen one of the neighborhood kids had accused him of cheating at some game they were playing. Nathan had tackled him and put him in a head lock.

Nathan was stronger than me when he was angry, like the Hulk, and I hadn't been able to pull him off. I panicked, worried Nathan would kill the poor kid and then he'd spend the rest of his life in prison. I should've gone to find a grown up, a cop, anyone other than our tiny wisp of a neighbor, but I'd run to her, out of breath and red-faced, begging her to help bring Nathan back from the edge of homicide.

She raced across the street with me, screamed Nathan's name and he'd paused mid-punch. She put her hand on his shoulder and he let the kid fall to the pavement. She grabbed his hand and he'd followed her back to our house. I didn't know how she did it. I didn't know if she held magic or if Nathan simply loved her that much. Either way, Savy was his salvation.

Which meant I needed to stop picturing her beautiful neck, and I needed to stop getting hard at the sound of her laughter.

When we were younger, she was nothing more than a neighbor kid who came to play with my brother—the only neighbor kid that came to play with my brother. Her role suited me fine. I was busy after our dad died. I threw myself into every after-school activity possible. I wanted the Deacon brothers to be remembered for something good, something other than a dead father, and an emotionally unstable son.

Then, the older Savy got, the more I noticed her in ways that were more than friendly. I'd kept my budding crush at bay for years. I'd told myself over and over she was a kid, and that she was my brother's best friend.

Hell, more than that, she was his whole world in every way, except they weren't together. Not like I wanted to be with her. Nathan needed her to navigate life.

Which meant she wasn't for me.

"Hey, college boy. You going to come swim with us or what?"

I opened one eye to see Savy grinning at me from our pool. The sun was bright and warm, no doubt the water would feel amazing. I wanted nothing more to join them. I'd only been home for a few days, but I couldn't help but notice Savannah had grown up since I'd been away at school.

She'd grown into her long legs, and she filled out her stark white swimsuit top spectacularly. She was eighteen now, and I swear she got sexier every time I saw her. I'd finished my sophomore year at a college two states away. Nathan and Savy graduated high school mere days ago.

"Shouldn't you two be out at a graduation party or something?"

Savy threw her head back and laughed. Yep, it was even more tempting than the image I'd had in my head only minutes before. "Right. Like I'd ever get this one to go to an actual party. Come on, it's Saturday, come play with us."

Her words went straight to my dick like a zap of unwanted electricity.

Savy was Nathan's girl. Not romantically. I've never once seen them approach anything close to sexual intimacy. But he loved her. She was so off limits it wasn't even funny. If my brother lost Savy, it'd destroy him. If he lost her to me, it'd destroy us all.

"All right, all right." I got up and dove into the pool. When I surfaced I felt Nathan's gaze on me, watching, scrutinizing, always studying. Did he see the lust in my eyes I tried so carefully to hide? "So, bro, did you pick a school yet?" Nathan was crazy smart. He could pretty much go anywhere he wanted on a full academic scholarship. If he wasn't so damned dark and unfriendly, he would've been homecoming king and student council president.

Like me.

He cocked his head to the side and stepped closer to Savy, making waves bank against my chest. "Sav is going to Emerson, so I think I might go with her."

Savy groaned and splashed water in his direction. "You are so frustrating. You want to go to Yale. We both know that. You're brilliant. Emerson is a small liberal arts school. There's no reason for you to go there." She turned to me, hands on her slender hips, water sliding down her cleavage I wanted to lick away. "Right Jeremy?" Was that pleading I saw in her eyes? She seemed to be communicating more than a simple conversation. "Tell him he needs to go to Yale."

I didn't like coming between Savy and Nathan, no one did. It never ended well. But I was finding it near impossible to deny her anything, even when I knew better. Especially since it appeared she wanted me to help her out.

"Yale is a really great school Nathan. Do you know how many kids dream of going there? It's not that far away. You'll still get to see Savy all the time." I kept my attention on him, watching every nuance in his facial expression to make sure I hadn't pissed him off by taking her side. Not that Nathan had ever or would ever hurt me, but he'd give me the cold shoulder, a full-blown silent treatment like no one's business.

Out of the corner of my eye I saw Savy glance back and forth between us, and then roll her eyes when she saw Nathan's smile disappear. She swam over to him and punched him teasingly on the arm. "Jer is right, Nate. We'll still see each other. You know Yale is the best choice for you."

Her gaze found mine, and what I saw made my chest tighten. Desperation and fear. It'd been only a flash, a quick glimpse that disappeared in an instant. Then her smile slipped firmly back into place as she ruffled Nathan's hair. "Hey. Who knows what life holds for you? Maybe, since you won't have me around all the time cramping your style, you'll find a girlfriend." There was humor in her tone, she was being self-deprecating to soothe him. No way could she believe she was "cramping" his style.

We both knew that Nathan didn't want anyone else.

I laughed too, following her lead, trying to take the edge off what she'd said. Trying to lessen the sting I'm sure he felt. Trying like hell to forget the terrified look I'd seen flash in her eyes.

"Yeah Nathan, a smart chick with those hot black framed glasses. I'm sure girls at Yale find geniuses like you irresistible." Not that girls here didn't. I'd seen them checking him out. I'd seen the yearning written all over their faces. He was dark, brooding, and he rarely spoke to anyone other than Savy. The other girls were all curious. They wanted to be the one to crack his shell. To break him. Little did they know that he'd been born broken.

Nathan grabbed Savy's arm, lightly, like she was made of glass. He pulled her to his side, hugging her to his chest. He at me looked over her head as he spoke, "I don't need anyone else, Sav. You don't cramp my style."

Sad, but true. For Nathan. But, it seemed, not for Savy. He sure as shit cramped hers.

Savy had never even been on a date, not that I'd noticed or heard about. She was gorgeous, smart, and sweet. Tons of guys had been interested over the years, but Nathan's quick temper and violent streak had kept everyone away.

I'd never thought to help her out, to try to get Nathan to loosen the reins. Honestly, I didn't want her dating anyone else either. She was too good for all those douche bags at our school. But now I couldn't stop staring at her round little ass or the way her bikini top looked much tighter than last summer. Her long blonde hair floated around her in the water, like she was a sexy mermaid.

For the first time, I began to wonder what *Savy* wanted. I wondered if she wanted to date, and if there'd ever been anyone she was interested in. More than anything, I wondered why I'd never really thought much about her wants and needs before this moment.

"All right, Nate. You've got to get ready for work." Savy patted Nathan on the chest and then swam away. "I promised my dad I would go through some boxes in the attic to see if there was anything I wanted up there. He's on another one of his organizational purges."

Nathan sighed, paddling after her. "Sav, I told you to wait. I'll help you do that tomorrow. You don't need to be in that attic alone, lifting all those boxes." Nathan had always been this way where Savy's safety was concerned, ever since we were little kids. All the parents thought it was endearing. Now it sounded kind of suffocating.

When I'd begun to crush on her over the last year, I fantasized about sneaking her out of the house after everyone was asleep. I'd take her to the lake, turn the stereo up loud and put every vice known to man in front of her and let her go crazy. If only for one night.

I'd kiss her under the stars, until we were both breathless and the windows in my car were fogged up. It was lame as far as fantasies went, but Savy seemed almost too pure to think about doing anything more.

She waved away his concern and then floated on her back next to the pool steps. "Ah, remember, I told you, I already put it off too long. What do you think are in those boxes? Bricks and snakes? I'll be fine."

"I can help you." The words tumbled out of my mouth before my brain checked in.

I'd never hung out with Savy without Nathan around, but since I'd been home, I was desperate to be alone with her. I wanted to know her. The *real* Savannah. The one that existed without Nathan.

I wanted to know if that quick flash of desperation had been my imagination. I looked over at my baby brother and saw his jaw was clenched and his eyes were flat and cold. Hell, the temperature in the pool had dropped a few degrees. Obviously, he didn't love the idea,

Sighing and rolling my eyes, I acted like I was doing him a favor. "I mean, if you're so worried about her hurting herself, I can help."

Eggshells. We were always walking on fucking eggshells around Nathan. The sad part: until I went away to college I'd never realized how exhausting it was. I'd been constantly trying to counterbalance him when we were in school together. He'd get in a fight? I'd run for class office. He'd get suspended? I'd make all state. One of us needed to be well liked and "normal." All that fell on me.

Savy didn't wait for Nathan's reaction to my offer as I would have. "That's really nice of you. Thanks." She kicked some water at Nathan. "Happy now? I have a babysitter."

My brother looked anything but happy. I stayed in the pool, watching the two of them talk. Savy worked hard to get him to laugh, breaking the underlying tension.

When he smiled, he looked like a freaking GQ model. He was dark inside and out. Dark hair, dark eyes, perpetually tanned skin. His hair was always purposefully mussed, and his smooth skin shaved clean. He looked good, and he did it only for her.

I'd always been told that Nathan and I looked so much alike we could've been twins.

I didn't see it, not really. Our personalities were too different. We were polar opposites. I always felt like our differences were stark and glaring, overshadowing any chance we had of looking like brothers.

Chapter Two

Savy

I'd known the Deacon boys for most of my life. I'd met them when I was six, Nate was seven but we were in the same class. Jeremy had been nine, and too older brother cool to hang out with us. I'd loved them both from the moment we met. I'd been *in* love with one of them forever. For years I'd fought it, I'd begged and pleaded with my stubborn heart. It'd be so much easier on everyone if it was Nate who gave me butterflies. Unfortunately, for all of us, it had always been Jeremy. He was easy going, quick to laugh, innately kind, and so incredibly gorgeous.

Well, they were both hot as all get out. Both brothers had extraordinarily deep brown eyes and dark shaggy hair. Where Nate had hard lines that made him look like a man, Jeremy had this baby face that girls swooned over. When I was younger I used to have this recurring dream: Jeremy would come to my window and wake me with a kiss. He would tell me to pack a bag and that we were running away. That we were going somewhere where we could be together, on an adventure. When I would wake up, I'd cry. I had wanted so badly for it to be true. I kept on crying because the guilt I felt for wanting to run away from Nate was overwhelming.

I'd never asked to be Nate's keeper. No one had ever asked if I wanted to be his reason for living: his reason for fighting the darkness.

Nate wasn't a sociopath. His parents had taken him to psychiatrists and had him tested and evaluated to be sure. He seemed to fall between lots of different diagnoses. One didn't fit, but a lot came close. He wasn't violent toward the people he loved. He was capable of love, and he *did* love. Nate didn't understand social norms, like someone with Asperger's, but not. He was socially appropriate with me and his family, and he didn't display any of the other diagnostic indications. It was more like he was perpetually cranky and had the shortest fuse in the history of the world. He didn't have any tolerance for…well, anything.

He hit first and asked questions later. I'm guessing here: not because he wanted to hurt people, but because he didn't understand them. He had a switch, and it seemed he could flip it on and off at will. He could either care, or not. Portray empathy, or not. As it turned out, he usually opted for not.

I never asked Nate about his feelings or the way he saw the world. I'd been so young when we met, and I accepted him for exactly who he was. I wasn't sure why I didn't question him more as we got older, his whims and moods affected my entire life.

I had never been on a real date except for one guy my freshman who'd stolen a kiss under the bleachers. Nate punched him in the nose, twice, shattering it. I had a flirty little thing going with a guy from my English Lit class, the only one I didn't share with Nate. He saw a text from him on my phone while I was in the shower. He'd blocked the guy's number and the next day the poor kid had a black eye.

After that, word was out. Don't look at Savy, don't talk to Savy. She was off limits, unless you wanted to get a beatdown from Nathan Deacon.

Now, four years later, I was worn out, my nerves were shot, and I needed a break. Nate was emotionally exhausting. It took everything in me to keep him level, and by now, there was nothing left for me.

I was elated and terrified of spending the evening in the attic with Jeremy. I'd never been alone with him. Nate was always there. Even when he wasn't, Jeremy and I had never thought to hang out without him. Probably because neither of us wanted to deal with the inevitable fallout. Nate would never take his anger out on me, but he would punish his brother one way or another.

"Savannah, honey, Uh, Jeremy is here." I could hear the question in my mom's voice as she called up the stairs to my room. Jeremy had been over to my house a hundred times, but never without Nate standing between us.

"I'm upstairs." I checked my hair in the mirror and quickly swiped on some lip gloss. I turned in time to see him reach the top of the stairs, his hand resting on the banister. I swear he got better looking every time I saw him. He was turning into a man, filling out, gaining confidence. Plus it seemed that every time he came home, he'd acquired a new tattoo. All through high school, Jeremy was all prep. After being in college, he changed. It seemed he cared less about being the perfect kid.

I could understand that. I could see where being away from his brother would change him. He didn't have to run interference for Nate at home and school. Jeremy no longer needed to be the perfect son to make up for all the aggravation Nate caused their parents. As much as I tried to fight it, as potentially *dangerous* I knew it was, my crush on Jeremy grew with every new encounter.

I smiled, blinking at the handsome guy standing before me. "Hey, thanks for coming to help. You didn't have to, but thank you nonetheless."

He shrugged like it was no big deal. "I didn't have any plans tonight, and we both know, if I hadn't agreed to help you Nathan would have called in sick to work." He stepped into my bedroom and plopped down on my bed.

Oh my gosh. Jeremy Deacon was on my bed.

My fifteen-year-old self was losing her mind right now.

"How long has Nathan been working at that gym over on Main?"

I sat next to him, trying to seem unaffected and cool, but probably coming off as nervous and fidgety. "A few months."

"That's just what the world needs, Nathan getting stronger." Jeremy lifted his arm to make a muscle. "Guess I'll have to bulk up now too." He sighed. "Or I'll never be able to take him."

Jeremy was ripped and was strong in his own right, but he wasn't bulky like Nate. Unfortunately, I understood what Jeremy meant. It was already hard enough to control Nate when his temper flared. The stronger he got, the less likely it was someone would be able to *physically* pull him back from the brink.

"He's been good. Keeping to himself, keeping calm. He's been going to see Dr. Briggs twice a week."

Jeremy snorted and got to his feet. "He hasn't been keeping to himself. Mom told me what happened at graduation practice. You don't have to make excuses for him to me. I know my brother."

I winced at the memory of what happened. I'd been the voice in Nate's head for ten years, and trying to downplay his actions was second nature. "That was one time, other than that he's been doing really well." I could hear the defensiveness in my tone, and I didn't even know why I bothered.

Someone had cracked a joke about Nate making it to graduation without having to be committed. Nate overheard. I had been all the way across the bleachers, and before I could get to him Nate had the guy pinned against a wall. Luckily, Nate hadn't hit him, so he didn't get expelled.

It was a miracle Nate was never kicked out of school for good. He'd been suspended a few times, and he'd been in detention so often they should've named the room after him. For the most part, he made sure to keep most of his violence off of school grounds. It helped that we lived in a small town. Everyone felt sorry for the Deacon boys for losing their father so young. It was as if the whole damn world gave Nate an excuse to misbehave while giving him a wide berth, and used me as foam batting on his rough edges.

"Come on." Jeremy held his hand out to me. Surprised, I took it and let him help me to my feet. He'd never touched me on purpose before. My heart went into hyper drive. "Savannah Nightingale, you are a saint and Nathan's lucky to have you."

I dropped his hand like it was on fire and walked past him toward the entrance to the attic. His comment irritated me. I didn't need any pity hand holds from my best friend's older brother, no matter how long I'd been dreaming of the day he would do it.

"Nate doesn't *have* me. It's everyone else who's lucky, right? As long as I'm around no one has to worry about him."

I didn't know what made me say that. Maybe because for the first time, in a really long time, I was alone with another human being. My parents and Nate's mom never saw anything wrong with us being joined at the hip. Somewhere along the way, everyone had made a tacit agreement that I was Nate's buffer and shield.

They never saw that I was drowning.

"Savy, I didn't mean—"

I shook my head, forcing my irritation down deep where it belonged, where it'd lived for years festering. "It's fine." I reached up and pulled the long white rope, bringing the attic ladder down. I climbed up and turned on the light, then sat down in front of a stack of boxes my dad had put aside a few weeks ago.

The first one I opened had nothing but old bedsheets I didn't even recognize. "Ew. Why would I want to take these with me to school? Who wants to sleep on someone else's sheets?" I used my foot to shove that box to the side, making it the start of the donate pile.

Jeremy climbed up, crossing the space hunched over so he didn't hit his head on the low beams to sit next to me. He knocked his shoulder into mine, even that brief contact made me giddy. Two touches in one day. I was going to combust.

He opened the box in front of him. "Books. Looks like a box of really old dusty books."

I smiled and traced my fingers over the spine of a bound hard copy. "*The Great Gatsby*. One of my favorites. Keep."

Jeremy raised an eyebrow. "You already read this one. Why keep it?"

I laughed. "I already read *all* the books in that box. I like to keep the things that speak to me, and all those books mean something different. Different but equally as special."

Kind of like the Deacon Brothers. Nathan wasn't easy to love, but that didn't mean I'd ever stop.

Jeremy nodded and picked up the heavy box, moving it closer to the door. "Savy?"

"Yeah?" I was digging through a small box full of pictures. They were of my parents and me mostly, with a few of Jeremy and Nathan mixed in.

"Can I ask you something?"

I held out the photo in my hand, one of their parents with mine, it was taken a few months before his dad passed away. A few months before my whole life had been turned upside down. "Of course."

He took the picture and sat down next to me, smiling, tracing his thumb over his dad's handsome face. I knew he missed his father like crazy, they both did, and with good reason. Mr. Deacon was one of the good ones. "Do you want Nathan to go to Emerson with you next year?"

I closed up the box and pushed it further into the attic. I didn't want all those pictures, but they sure as hell didn't need to get thrown away either. "No."

I opened the next box, which was full of stuffed animals. I kicked it toward the giveaway pile, the sound of it sliding across the floor grating my ears. I turned and looked at Jeremy, really let myself look at him. Which was not something I usually let myself do in case someone saw me swoon. Holy crap, he was gorgeous, and no lie, I might embarrass myself in public.

His eyes held nothing but curiosity. He wasn't afraid of my answer, he wasn't terrified that I'd say no and he'd be left to deal with the fallout. That made me want to keep talking, to tell him everything I'd been feeling. It felt like he was lending me his quiet strength, which gave me what I needed to speak my reality.

"Do you want to know the truth?"

He swallowed, his gaze still on mine, unwavering. "Yeah."

I felt my eyes fill with tears, and I dug my nails into my palms trying to keep them at bay. "I need a break, Jer." One tear escaped, and I wiped it away quickly. "I love Nate, you know I do, but I'm so tired of being his compass. His warden. I'm so tired of making sure he doesn't get into fights or mouth off to a teacher. Going away to school without Nate is going to be so scary, but I need this. I'm ready for it. I want to go to parties. I want to date. I want to get into trouble. Not spend all my time keeping Nate out of it."

More tears spilled free. Before I could wipe them away, Jeremy reached up and brushed them off my face with the back his knuckles. He left his hand on my cheek, the warmth from his touch seeping down into my tired soul.

"You deserve that Savy. You deserve that and more." His thumb kept wiping at my seemingly never-ending tears. "I always assumed you were okay. I assumed that you were happy with being Nathan's keeper. I guess we all did."

I resisted the urge to drop my gaze to my lap. This was the longest I'd ever looked into Jeremy's eyes and it was making butterflies take flight in my stomach. "I was. I am. When we were younger, when your dad was alive…" I took a deep breath. "Nate was different. He was lighter, he was—"

"Easier." Jeremy took his hand off my cheek and it made me want to cry harder for the loss. "Well, less violent anyway."

I nodded, swallowing past the lump in my throat. "Yeah. I mean he always had a short fuse, and he'd always let words and emotions fly, but when your dad was still here, he knew how to handle him."

Jeremy put his hand on my thigh. In our whole lives, he had never touched me as much as he had in the last thirty minutes. And I was craving more. "When my dad died it became you. You were the only one who could calm him down. Bring his mood back to center."

I shrugged. "I was so young. All I knew was that I could make my best friend smile when he was feeling sad. By the time I realized what was happening, how much Nate needed me to stay even—"

"You couldn't leave him to fend for himself. We relied on you, all of us."

All of us. That was the problem, wasn't it? I was a child, and all the adults in Nathan's life had no problem using me. A sad truth, and Jeremy realizing it made it all so glaringly obvious. I was suddenly so angry I stood and started pacing the attic, my head bent to keep from whacking it on the beams.

"Do you know I've never gone to a slumber party? I tried *once*. I was having so much fun. It was really late, and we were all up watching movies when my parents came and got me. Nate had a nightmare and he wouldn't stop screaming for me." I shook my head. "I was fucking twelve. Your mom was hysterical and my parents made me leave a sleepover to take care of your brother. How fucked up is that?"

Jeremy's eyes went wide. "I never knew that. I also never knew you dropped the f bomb so freely."

I snorted. "You don't know anything about me Jeremy Deacon. Your brother doesn't share." I wiped my eyes and sat back down. "I've been kissed once in my entire life."

Jeremy laughed at that. "Sloan Smith. I remember. Nathan kicked his ass."

I jerked back, my tone biting and so completely unlike me. "Is that funny to you?"

"Actually that one *is* funny, Sloan was a player, not to mention a douche. You could do better." Jeremy looked at the ground. "I always kind of wondered if maybe, you know, you and Nathan…"

"Really? Me and Nate? No. Not even once." Nathan had never tried. He'd hold my hand, kiss my head and my cheek, we'd cuddle in bed like brother and sister. That was it. I took a deep breath. "Eighteen-year-old virgin with no friends. College is going to be a breeze, huh?"

"I'm your friend."

"No you aren't."

I wanted what he said to be true, but it wasn't. I wanted Jeremy to be more than my friend. I wanted him to be my everything. I wanted to open my mouth and ask him to kiss me. Ask him to show me what it felt like to be touched, to be held. But I couldn't do that, I couldn't come between him and his brother. Nate was possessive of my time and my attention. We weren't dating, we'd never even came close. But I knew he felt a kind of ownership over me. It was part of who he was and how he was with me. I didn't necessarily like it, but I understood he needed it to feel safe.

Jeremy placed his hand back on my thigh, using his hold to turn me toward him. "I want to be."

My eyes searched his. I didn't know if it was because we were alone for the first time, or because I was leaving for college in a couple of months. Maybe it was because he knew my secret—knew how miserable I really was. Maybe it was the way the sun was setting through the round attic window, bathing everything in an orange glow. Maybe it was how good he smelled, and how handsome he was.

When his gaze dipped lower to my lips, I leaned in. His right hand tightened on my thigh and his left hand moved back to my cheek. I closed my eyes.

"Savy."

His lips were a breath away from mine. "Jeremy," I whispered his name, chills breaking out all over my skin.

I wanted to be kissed, I needed to be kissed. This one stolen moment where it was only Jeremy and me. I needed this teeny tiny little taste of freedom, and I prayed he would give it to me.

Chapter Three

Jeremy

The way she said my name was the most amazing sound I'd ever heard. She was asking me to kiss her, begging me actually. Oh how I wanted to. I wanted to kiss Savy more than I should. I couldn't do that to her or to Nathan.

"Savy, I…" I pulled back, untangling my hand from her shiny blonde hair. I infused my voice with insanely upbeat positivity, like I was about to host my own Ted Talk. "I want to be your friend. I know it's been tough with Nathan, and you've taken on more than anyone should ever have to. We have two months of summer vacation ahead of us. Let's hang out. I'll take you to some parties, introduce you some people."

I'm gonna to try real fucking hard not to kiss you or let my brother find out.

If he found out, he'd crush her with his bare hands. Figuratively speaking.

Nathan loved Savy, and he needed her in his life in a way that most people would never understand. I'd watched them for years, and even I had trouble wrapping my mind around their connection. She was his whole world, and as unfair as it was, she was the one who kept it spinning.

"Friends? You want to be my friend for two months?" Her eyes narrowed with confusion, and probably disappointment.

Listening to her repeat it back to me made me realize how weak it sounded. I'd basically offered a friendship with an expiration date. "Yeah. It'll be fun." I stood quickly, to keep myself from touching her tempting skin again. "What are you doing tomorrow?"

She shrugged, looking a bit defeated, which tugged at my heart strings. "Tomorrow's Sunday, so not much."

"A bunch of people are gathering down at the lake. Sunday Funday." I put my hands on my hips, sending her what I hoped was a friendly smile. "Come with me." I knew Nathan worked tomorrow, my mom still kept a family calendar on the refrigerator. I wasn't attempting to sneak around with Savy. I was simply using the free day to our advantage. I wasn't lying. I was employing good time management.

"Will there be a lot of people there?" She looked down and played with the hem of her faded t-shirt. Seemingly nervous and timid at the idea of being around a bunch of people she didn't know. All of whom she'd had class with over the last twelve years.

"The lake on a Sunday usually draws a big crowd." How had she never been to a lake party? It was a rite of passage in this town. My little brother had kept Savy under lock and key for too long. She'd graduated, but she'd yet to experience high school. I couldn't change the past, and I wouldn't dare try to alter her future, but I could do this. I could help her live in the present. "I'll be right next to you the whole time. Promise."

"Okay."

"Yeah?"

She nodded her head, a glowing expression of resolve coming over her beautiful face. "Yeah."

Neither one of us mentioned Nathan for the rest of the evening. We kept the conversation light and superficial while we went through the rest of the boxes in the attic. I kept my hands to myself while I helped her haul the "keep" pile down to the garage, and then I took the trash to the curb.

I was home for the summer, and I'd spend it walking a tight rope around my baby brother once again. But I could do this. I could be Savy's friend. I'd help her, and I'd make sure Nathan didn't get hurt in the process.

Then, I'd head back to college where life was so much easier.

***

"How'd it go with Sav?" I glanced up to find Nathan leaning against my door, his shoulder on the frame and his arms crossed. He was ripped, His muscles bulged against the sleeves of his work polo.

I looked back down at the book I was reading, *The Great Gatsby*. "It went fine." I'd never read the story in high school. I didn't read anything unless someone made me. I wasn't naturally brilliant like Nathan. I was more jock. Long distance running got me into college, not my brains.

"Did you finish, or do I need to go over there tomorrow morning before work?"

I was afraid to meet his eyes a second time. I was afraid that he'd see the guilt, see the memory of our almost kiss. "No, we finished. There weren't all that many boxes." I took a deep breath and tore my eyes away from the hardback Savy had lent me. "I took the ones she wanted to keep down to the garage and the ones she wanted to throw out to the trash. All done." I smiled.

He nodded. "Thanks for helping her. You really didn't have to do that."

Meaning he really didn't *want* me to do that. Possessive nut-job. I say that with mostly love in my heart. Nathan wasn't crazy, not really. But he definitely had a personality disorder no shrink had been able to pinpoint. He was dark and moody and his emotions tended to spiral quickly. He sure as fuck didn't like people. It was as if he'd been born into the body of a 'roided out jock mixed with a crotchety old man. My dad hadn't wanted Nathan to be medicated, but back then, when Dad was still with us, Nathan hadn't been that bad.

I shrugged, like me offering to even help Savy in the first place was no big deal. "I didn't have anything else to do."

"About that, what are your plans this summer? You want me to see if I can get you a job at the gym?" He shifted his stance, uncrossing his arms and shoving his hands into his pockets.

Did he just call me lazy? I trained year round, took a full class load each semester, and worked in the trainer's office at the field house during the off season. This summer I was taking three online courses to get ahead and shadowing a massage therapist in town. Maybe Nathan wanted to make sure I didn't have any extra time to help Savy with household chores.

"With training and classes, I don't think I'd have much time for a job this summer."

Not to mention that neither of us actually *had* to work. When our dad passed away, we'd gotten an inheritance plus a settlement that came from the pharmacy that'd screwed up his cholesterol medication. That one mistake had caused his massive stroke and lead to his untimely death. I worked at the trainer's office to help pad my resumé for after-college employment.

I wasn't too sure why Nathan was choosing to spend precious time away from Savy when he didn't have to. I glanced back down at my book, hoping he'd get the hint and go away. I was actually digging this Fitzgerald guy's writing.

"You want to go for a run in the morning?"

I raised an eyebrow in surprise. "For real?" I'd been a runner from the moment I'd perfected walking. Nathan had never taken an interest, and he'd never once asked to run with me. He always preferred weights to endurance, as evidenced by his ridiculously bulging muscles.

He shrugged. "I've been running with Sav in the mornings. She's really gotten into it and it's not safe for her to go alone."

I resisted the urge to roll my eyes at his overprotectiveness. We lived in a freaking gated neighborhood, and Savy was eighteen years old. It was more than safe for her to run alone. Yet another example of my brother smothering her.

"Yeah, sure. Thanks for the invite."

He shrugged again before walking away.

That was the most I'd talked to my brother in the last six months. We texted every once in a while, but we never chatted on the phone. I rarely came home to visit. When I'd gotten away, gone to college, I realized how hard it was living in this house. Watching Nathan for signs of stress. Being careful what we said in front of him. I was selfish. I knew that. But I'd needed a break and being away at school had become the perfect excuse. Which was exactly what was on Savy's mind these days. Going to school, and getting away.

I tried to keep reading, but couldn't seem to concentrate anymore. I clicked off the lamp on my bedside table and stared at my ceiling. The fan was on, cutting through the shadows from the streetlight. Today had taken a turn, and my summer was completely altered because of it. I was looking forward to spending time alone with Savy. I wanted to know her. The *her* that existed without Nathan attached to her side, and demanding every minute of her time and energy.

My cell vibrated, lighting up on the mattress beside me.

Thanks for helping me tonight. You're the best.

Savy had my number for emergencies. You know, in case Nathan lost his shit and one of us needed back-up. This was the first time she texted me. Seeing her name on the screen was making me smile like a fucking fool.

I'm glad we got to hang out.

I really was. I was *too* glad. I'd liked being alone with Savy way more than I had any right to. Damn, I'd wanted to kiss her so fucking bad. She smelled like flowers, and bubble gum lip gloss.

It was nice of you to invite me to the lake tomorrow. I don't want you to feel obligated to follow through with it. I was having a little mini meltdown. It isn't really all that bad.

Yes it was. She was a freaking prisoner in her life, and my brother was the cell she was living in. That girl needed a break. No one would be able to understand that like I did. I got away, and it wasn't until I had that I realized how stifling life with Nathan could be. Savy needed to be young and crazy and wild. All things that would cause Nathan to lose his shit.

Are you kidding? You'll be doing me a favor by coming. With you by my side I won't look like some lame college guy at a high school party.

I was mostly kidding. A lot of my friends were already home for the summer and there wasn't much else to do around here on a Sunday other than drink at the lake.

Do people swim there? Should I wear a suit?

Hell yeah. Wear the bikini you had on earlier today.

As soon as I hit send my heart stopped beating, and time stood still. Did I just flirt with Savy on a text? Was I off my fucking rocker? I told her I'd be her *friend*. I should be telling her to wear sweatpants, not a sexy two piece. I closed my eyes and banged my skull against the headboard a few times, groaning at my rash stupidity.

"You need something, man?" I opened my eyes to find my brother back in my doorway, the light from the hall making him an imposing dark shape backlit enough for me to see his face.

I shook my head. "Nope. All good." He narrowed his eyes, watching me. My phone vibrated on the bed. My heart stopped again. I was going to end up having a heart attack by the end of this text conversation. I looked down, sighing in relief when I saw the damn thing was face down on the mattress.

"You sure you're okay?"

I nodded. "I'm greeeeeeat." I imitated Tony the Tiger, like the commercials from when we were kids. *Why?* Sheer nervousness.

His eyes narrowed further, but his lips twitched. The lip twitch was pretty much all anyone but Savy could get by way of a smile out of him. "'Night."

"'Night, Nathan."

I waited until I heard his bedroom door shut before I picked my phone up and opened Savy's latest text.

You got it. See you tomorrow afternoon.

I'd told her I'd pick her up around noon, which was when Nathan would be leaving for work. Yeah, I was a bastard. I could tell myself I wasn't sneaking around behind my brother's back with Savy all I wanted, but it wouldn't make it true.

Nathan invited me to run with you guys in the morning.
You didn't tell him about the party, did you?

That poor girl. Nathan wasn't her dad, he wasn't her brother, and he wasn't her boyfriend. Him knowing she wanted to go have fun without him terrified her, and was fucking sad. I felt trapped by my brother and his moods growing up, but never once did I have to curb my life to make him happy. But Savy did, every damn day of the last ten years.

No. I didn't say a word.

I'd lie for her a million times over.

They say two wrongs don't make a right, but that was feeling like utter bullshit. Savy had been wronged by me, my brother, and our parents.

I'd do whatever it took to start to right that.

Chapter Four

Savy

Nate didn't like to run. He never had. It'd always been Jeremy's thing. I thought when I decided to start running in the mornings, I'd get some exercise along with a little bit of alone time. Two mornings, two glorious mornings I'd had to myself. Only me and the rising sun. But then Nate had left early for work one Saturday and caught me jogging on the darkened streets of our neighborhood alone. That was the flipping end of that. It didn't matter how many times I told him I was fine, that I was safe. He insisted on joining me.

When I around thirteen I started having this recurring nightmare that I woke up on an operating table and Nate would be sewn to my side. I would start to cry but he'd be full of smiles, happy to spend the rest of his life joined to me at the actual hip. It didn't take a psychologist to figure out that one.

"Morning, boys." I smiled as both Deacon brothers jogged across the dew filled grass, Nate wearing a small grin and Jeremy wearing a huge beaming one. "I had no idea you were a runner, Savy." Jeremy held his hand up for me to high five.

"I started only a few months ago. You'll probably smoke me." I slapped his hand and then slung my arm playfully around Nathan's neck. "I'm faster than this guy, though."

"She's a natural, Jer." Nate kissed my temple, laughing. My day was made. I knew I'd been complaining about Nathan a lot over the last day or so. But I *did* love him. He was my best friend. He didn't laugh often, so I counted each and every one of them like tiny treasures. The kiss? I was the only person Nate showed physical affection with, other than the random hug to our moms. Sometimes I wanted to protest, but after all this time, I wasn't sure how.

The three of us set off at an easy pace. Nothing but the sound of our shoes on the pavement and the birds waking up in the trees. After about five minutes I lengthened my stride, Jeremy effortlessly matched me. I knew he was holding back on my account. I'd been watching that boy run since he was in junior high. He was crazy talented. The two of us could easily leave Nate in the dust. He wasn't quick and didn't have our endurance, but neither one of us made a move to go any faster.

After our quick three mile run we'd headed through the side door, into my kitchen. My mom always had a fresh pot of coffee going for my dad as soon as she woke up. "You three reek." She held her nose as we shuffled past, sweating and fanning our flushed faces.

Jeremy leaned in and hugged her real tight, making her laugh. "Do we?"

I hid my smile behind my steaming mug of coffee. I'd forgotten how friendly and easy-going Jeremy was, how playful and happy. I spent all my time around Nate, the dark as night brother. Sure, I could get him to laugh and smile every once in a while, but it wasn't the norm. I felt like Jeremy was the sun and I'd been locked in a pitch black room for too long.

My mom swatted at him with a bright floral dish towel and handed each guy an oversized banana nut muffin. "What are you kids up to today? Anything fun?"

"I have to head into work." Nate took one last sip of his black coffee and then brushed another kiss to my temple. "I actually need to head home for a shower." He rubbed his hand down my back, making me blush when I realized Jeremy was watching our every interaction. I didn't ask for the touches, but I didn't stop him either. "See you tonight?"

I nodded. "Have a good day."

"You coming, man?" Nate paused with his hand on the back door, looking to his older brother.

My gaze shifted to Jeremy once again. I didn't want him to leave. I wanted to steal another few seconds in his light, which made guilt start to claw at my insides with razor sharp talons. "I'm going to finish my coffee first. I'll be home in a bit." He shrugged like it was no big deal.

Before Nate could protest my mom spoke up, oblivious to the sudden tension in the room. "Come on, Nathan. I'll walk you over. I made some extra muffins for your mom." She threaded her arm through his and let him lead her out of the house.

Jeremy and I stood in silence for a few seconds. Both looking at our cups or around the room, anywhere but at each other. Finally Jeremy broke the quiet. "You two seem like an old married couple. You know that, right?" He was leaning against the butcher block island in the middle of my kitchen chowing down happily on a fresh baked muffin and getting crumbs all over his shirt.

"I'm well aware. Thank you." I grabbed a muffin off the cooling rack, since my mom hadn't bothered to hand me one. I took a large bite and then ranted around a mouthful of delicious muffin, "You know what's really messed up?" I didn't give him a chance to answer. "My parents are okay with it." I pointed at him with the muffin still in my hand. "You know they've never even asked me if Nate and I are dating."

His eyebrows shot up. "Really?"

"Yeah. Nathan fell asleep in my bed one night and we didn't wake up until my dad came to tell me to get ready for school." I took another big bite. "You know what my dad said when he found us?" Once again, I didn't give Jeremy time to guess. "He said, *Oh uh hey guys, It's time for school.* Then he turned around and walked out."

"What did you expect him to say?" Jeremy popped the last bite of muffin into his mouth then wiped the crumbs on his sweaty shirt.

"I don't know, how' bout *What are you doing in my daughter's room? What are you doing in her bed?*" I shook my head. "But not my dad. Even he was too afraid to cross Nate, to upset the balance."

"I don't think I've ever seen you angry before." Jeremy grinned a wicked little smirk. "I think I love it."

I threw my hands in the air. "When the hell do I have time to be angry? I spend all my time making sure Nate never gets angry. Oh no, don't let the Hulk out." I shook my head. "I'm like the freaking other Avenger who is always calming the Hulk?"

"Black Widow?"

"Yeah, her. The one with the setting sun lullaby." I took a deep breath, closed my eyes and tried to calm my temper. A temper I never knew I possessed. A temper that only seemed to come out around Jeremy.

It was like a dam had broken last night in my attic. There was another soul who knew my truth and now I couldn't stop spouting it.

Guilt took hold of my gut, my heart beginning to ache from the terrible things I was saying out loud about Nate. "I'm sorry. That was rude. I love your bother. He's my best friend. I'm lucky to have him. Lucky that we have each other." There. That was more my usual speed. I nodded, please with myself for reigning my latest angry outburst.

Jeremy suddenly pushed off the island and stepped closer, his spicy scent surrounding me and stealing all thoughts from my brain. Even his sweat was alluring. "That's bullshit."

I shook my head. "No. It's the truth. He really is my best friend." We'd been through so much together, and it wasn't all bad. We'd also had a lot of fun, a lot of good memories. I shouldn't tarnish that. It wasn't fair to either of us. I didn't know what had come over me lately. Maybe I was the actual Hulk. Or Mr. Hyde.

He snorted. "He's your *only* friend." He took another step toward me. "You haven't had a day off since my father died. You've been babysitting Nathan for years. You said you were tired, didn't you?"

I swallowed, backing into the countertop, afraid to say it out loud again. Once was enough.

"Don't you want to break out? Don't you want to have fun? Go crazy and live a little?" Jeremy took another step, I had nowhere else to go. He rested his chest against mine. I looked up into his dark eyes, my heart pounding out a wild rhythm. "Don't you want to be the bad one for a change?"

Chapter Five

Jeremy

Holy hell. What was I doing? *Don't you want to be the bad one for a change?* I shouldn't've said that to her. I should have listened to her throw her little fit and then been sympathetic. That's what a friend would do. That's what I'd intended to do. Up until she'd backtracked and started gushing all that *I love my best friend* crap. I wasn't going to let her take it all back. I wasn't going to let her stuff all her hurt and frustration back inside like she'd never let it out in the first place.

She was Nathan's salvation, and I was going to be hers. At least for the next two months.

I jutted my chin over my shoulder. "Go change. It's time for the lake." I needed her to move away from me, because I didn't have the willpower to take a step back. She was too gorgeous, and she smelled too enticing.

Savy stared at me, her chest heaving, and my fingers itched to touch her. "Go." She finally looked down at her tennis shoes, breaking eye contact at my demand and walked past me toward the stairs.

When she was out of sight I let out a sigh of relief. There was no doubt in my mind, I wanted her. I wanted to watch her fall apart in my arms. I wanted to be the only one who got to see her let loose, let go. My desire for her was close to overriding all the reasons I knew I needed to stay away.

***

"When did you get this car?"

Savy had the passenger window down, and her blonde hair was blowing in the breeze. "When I went away to school I left Nathan the Tahoe." I gripped the steering wheel, trying really hard not to let her affect me. Trying to keep my eyes on the road and not the bikini top peeking out of her demure sundress. "I saw this parked outside the student union and had to have it." I reached out and petted the dash of my 1969 Dodge Charger. I'd always wanted a muscle car.

"I love it." She stroked the black leather seat next to her. "When did you start with the tattoos?"

I shrugged. "I wanted to get one to remember my dad." I pointed to the tat on the back of my arm, *love you kid*, in his handwriting. "But once I started, I couldn't seem to stop. It's addicting." I didn't need to be perfect at Northeastern University. I could be whoever I wanted to be now that I was away from my brother. I didn't have people to distract or a mom to make smile.

"Why didn't you come home last summer?"

"Why are you so nosy?" I glanced at her, smirking, letting her know I was kidding. The truth was that I loved the freedom and ease of life away from my family. But I was too much of a coward to admit that to her. I'd been enjoying myself while she'd been barely living. "Work. I, uh, shadowed our athletic trainer all last summer."

She nodded.

"What are the odds my brother will actually head to Yale next year?" I wanted the same for her. I wanted freedom for the beautiful girl sitting next to me. She deserved it. It was more than apparent she was craving it.

"Not good." She sighed sadly. "Unless I go too."

"Why Emerson?" I thought I knew the answer to this, it was in the way she made the school sound less than to Nathan. But I wanted to hear her say it out loud and admit it to herself.

"It's a good school, it's small. It's in Boston, which is one of my favorite cities." She looked out the window, holding her hand out into the breeze. "I didn't think Nate would follow me there. Not in a million years. A liberal arts school? There isn't anything for him at Emerson."

"Except you." I kept my eyes on the road as I spoke. "You'll be at Emerson and that's all he cares about."

She was silent for a few minutes before she spoke again. "I'm hoping I can still convince him to go to Yale. I'm hoping that you will help me. Your dad went to Yale, and I know that's why Nate applied."

"I'll do what I can. Okay?"

I'd try. I'd do everything I could to help my brother see that Boston wasn't the place for him. That he was destined for greatness and he needed to live up to his potential. I'd spout all that crap. I'd spout it 'til the cows came home. In the end though, it'd be Savy who'd have to put her foot down. We both knew it.

"Hey, if you really do end up at Emerson, we'll be neighbors." I went to Northeastern she'd basically live next door to me.

"I got into Northeastern too, but I figured if you and I were at the same school, there'd be no stopping Nate from joining us."

"I didn't know you applied to Northeastern." Not that I'd have any reason to know. It's not like we'd been besties before this weekend. We were constantly thrown together because of our families and her closeness with Nathan. For all our years of sharing my brother and propping him up, I'd spent more one-on-one time with Savy over this weekend than I had in my entire life. I knew it was selfish, but I'd been glad that Nathan had someone to occupy his time. Keep him calm. I wasn't going to do anything to upset the balance Savy helped maintain in our house. I always thought she was great: sweet and kind, but I was more than happy to leave Nathan's one and only friend to him.

"I applied everywhere."

"Except Yale." I made a left down the dirt road that led to the lakeshore.

"I got into Yale." Her voice was small and quiet, almost like she was afraid to say those words too loud. Afraid that somehow Nathan would hear her whispers from miles and miles away.

I glanced at her quickly, taking in the way her eyes were trained on her lap. "You got into Yale? That's a really big accomplishment, Savy. Congratulations."

She smiled. "Thanks."

Savy was brilliant, and she'd gotten into every school she'd applied to, even Yale. But she couldn't celebrate it. She couldn't shout her accomplishments from the rooftops. Nope. She had to whisper them inside the safety of my car. She was shrinking herself to get away from her best friend.

That was the saddest thing I'd heard yet.

I turned my attention back to the road and we drove the rest of the way in silence. I pulled up along the tree line and parked my car out of the way where it wouldn't get hit by some drunk kid trying to find their way out. The lake was crawling with people. There was a beer pong table, several mostly naked sun bathers, and two tapped kegs side-by-side. I'd been out here almost every weekend when I was in high school while Savy had spent every weekend at home doing whatever Nathan wanted to do.

"You ready to have some fun?"

I watched in fascination as she took in the chaos around her. The people, the booze, the music. She turned to me, a big grin on her pretty face. "Hell yeah."

To the best of my knowledge, Savy had never been to a real party. I'd never seen her out drinking stale beer with her peers. Nathan would've never agreed to it, and he never would've let her go alone.

I watched as she edged toward the crowd, her hands clasped in front of her like she wasn't sure what to do or how to act. I sipped my beer, at war with myself wondering if I should save her or let her figure this out for herself. I decided to let her be, let her navigate on her own.

What's that saying, teach a man to fish? Well, this was me, teaching Savy how to be a beautiful eighteen-year old-girl.

She kept glancing over her shoulder, wearing a nervous smile, like she was making sure I was still there. Making sure I hadn't abandoned her. I wouldn't leave her, but I wouldn't do this for her. She had it in her, I knew she did. She craved freedom, and I needed her to grasp it for herself.

She paused at the tapped keg, biting her bottom lip. I smiled as three different guys stepped up to her, offering to get her a drink. She was twisting her fingers, but she nodded and accepted a beer. She was pulled into a larger group, and she waved awkwardly at some people she seemed to recognize. I couldn't help but smile as I watched. Like a pretty fawn, taking her first steps, Savy was discovering her legs.

Fast forward, I was basically having to keep the dudes away with a baseball bat. Savy was playing beer pong with another bikini clad chick, and kicking ass. I sat on my buddy Max's tailgate, keeping a watchful eye on her. She was here to let loose and have fun, not lose her fucking virginity. Suddenly her newfound outgoing personality was less adorable and more worrisome.

Max came out of the woods with a brunette chick tucked under his arm and a satisfied smirk on his face. "Is that Savannah Nightingale?"

"Yep."

He sent his companion packing with a playful smack on her ass and then held his fist out for a bump. "Nathan know she's here?"

I handed him a cup of beer. Max and I had graduated together and had kept in touch even though we went to school on opposite coasts. He'd been one of my best friends in high school and I liked getting to see him on the rare occasions we were home at the same time. "Nope."

He winced. "He's going to kick your ass, bro." Max knew my brother. We'd been friends since the fourth grade. He knew how Nathan was with Savy, and how he was with everyone else. "You looking to lose a limb? Going after your brother's girl is a sure-fire way to do it."

"First, she's not my brother's girl. She's his best friend. Second, how do you know this is *my* doing?"

He laughed and slapped me on the back. "I remember what those two were like, and rumor is nothing's changed. Savannah doesn't talk to anyone besides Nathan. If anyone tries to get close to her, he gets pissed. The only person with enough balls to go against your brother at this point is you. The only semi-sane reason for you to go against him is if you're tapping that."

I shoved him to the side. "I'm not tapping that. Who the hell says that anymore?" Though, he did have a point. No one would go against Nathan, not even Savy until I'd convinced her to. "Savy needs to learn to party before she starts college, and Nathan is at work today."

I should feel guilty sneaking around behind my little brother's back. I sort of did, but Savy's admission in the car, the way she'd kept getting into Yale *and* Northeastern from him made some of that guilt evaporate. Savy needed to breathe. She needed my help.

"Besides, what he doesn't know won't kill him."

"No, but what he finds out might kill *you*."

I shot Max a look and then downed my lukewarm beer. "Then you better keep your mouth shut, yeah?" I hopped off the tailgate and headed in the direction of the keg. I decided to allow myself two beers. The last thing I needed was to get pulled over with Savy in the car.

I watched her while I refilled my cup. She was laughing with her hand on her bare stomach, the sound nothing short of pure magic. The guys were drawn to her like moths to a flame. They couldn't seem to look away. I should've gone back to Max. I should've sat my happy ass on his tailgate until Savy was ready to go home. But I didn't. Call me a moth.

"Looks like you're having a good time."

She reached out and rested her hand on my shoulder, her touch somehow making it hard to swallow. "I am having the best time, Jer. Thank you so much for bringing me." All the girls were in bikinis, but no one looked as good as Savy. She was tall and thin, her stomach flat and her hips narrow.

"You want to go for a swim?" The words spilled out of my mouth, unchecked. I couldn't take them back, could I?

"Yeah." She picked up her long blonde hair off her neck, fanning herself. "It's getting really hot out here."

I was getting hot too, and it had absolutely nothing to do with the weather. Savy's smiles, her newfound happiness, and her friendly touches were a deadly combination to my vow to be her friend and allow her a space to let loose.

We walked side-by-side down to the shoreline and waded in. Neither of us spoke as we both sank down to our knees, letting the cool water wash over our heated skin. Her hand brushed my stomach and I jerked back like I'd been shot.

"Sorry. I didn't mean…"

I shook my head. "No. I…didn't, uh, I thought you were a fish."

I thought you were a fish? Seriously? Come on, man.

"Crap. I left my drink on the table." She looked behind me, searching the shore.

"Here. You can have mine." Yep. Please put your lips where mine have been, because that won't make *not* touching you any harder. For the love of everything holy, I was a glutton for punishment.

"Thank you." I watched like a creeper as she took a sip from my cup, her mouth as it touched the cup's rim, then, as she took a sip, I was engrossed at the movement of her throat as she swallowed. I was hard as a rock underneath this water. I was going to have to stay in here until the sun went down.

She handed back my drink and our hands touched. I closed my eyes and bit the inside of my cheek. What was happening to me? I wasn't a kid. I'd been with tons of girls. I knew how to control myself. But fuck if Savy didn't turn me on with every little thing she did. Every smile, ever accidental touch, every stolen look. I was playing with fire. I'd set out today to let her have fun. Nothing more. But the longer I was around her, and the more she let down the walls she'd erected, the harder it was to resist.

"We should head home soon," I told her.

Her easy grin fell. "Oh, uh, okay."

"Nathan will be getting off work and I really don't want him to find out about this." God I sounded like a pussy, afraid of my younger brother. I kept teetering between not giving a fuck and fucking terrified. It was pathetic, and I knew it.

"I understand." She looked down and trailed her fingers through the water, the small ripples fanning outward until they faded back under the surface. "Thank you for doing this for me. I know what the consequences could be for you."

I hated taking away her joy. I hated I was ruining her fun, I hated that I'd shown her a glimpse of what life could be without Nathan and now I was delivering her back to him. I wanted so badly for things to be different. For all of us.

"I'm sorry," I muttered. I was sorry because I wished like hell I could do more, give her more.

"It's not so bad." She took my cup and drained it dry. "Nate isn't a monster. He's my best friend." She was back tracking again, letting her guilt override her sense of self-preservation. I wouldn't allow it.

Maybe I couldn't give her freedom, I couldn't give her back the years she'd lost, but I could give her a safe space where she didn't have to profess everything was okay when it wasn't. A space where her guilt didn't have to exist.

"You don't have to pretend around me. You can be you. You can be tired. You can be irritated and angry and willful. Be wild. Be reckless and loud. Complain, throw a fit. Scream, cry, laugh, curse. Do it all. You be the one to lose control for a change. I'll be right here to make sure you get it back."

That was the least I could do for her. Being my brother's keeper had put her in an emotional and social straight jacket. She deserved to be out of control, she deserved to be young. Our parents, and yes, me too, had kept her from being able to be a kid, a goofy tween, and a beautiful teenage girl. It was a wonder she hadn't combusted from the isolation.

I'd moved closer to her with every word I'd spoken until our chests were touching. I hadn't meant to get so close. It seemed my body had a mind of its own when it came to her.

She was breathing heavily, her face was flushed, and her lips were parted. Damn. She was excited and fuck if that didn't make my dick even harder. Her gaze searched mine, and she held me in a trance. I knew what she was waiting for and I wanted to give it to her so damn bad. I couldn't, so I looked over her shoulder, breaking the contact, too afraid of the consequences.

I heard her let out a small sigh. "Okay. I will," she murmured.

She stood and walked past me and out of the water like a freaking swimsuit model heading into the crowd of people dancing on the sandy shoreline. I watched as she made her way into the middle of the group and random guys touched her, danced with her and held her body. Someone handed her another beer and she drank it down fast.

I knew she wasn't trying to punish or tease me. She was only doing what I'd suggested she do. She was taking my advice. But she wound me tighter with every move she made. I was jealous of the guys who put their hands on her. I was enamored by the look on her face and the fun she was having. I wanted to be right there with her. Beside her. Claiming her as mine.

Damn it.

I could lead her to the good time, but I couldn't participate. She could lose control, but I couldn't. As long as I remembered that, we'd both be okay, we'd all survive this summer.

Eventually I made my way to the shore, I untangled her arms from some kid's neck and held her hand on the way back to my car.

She turned the radio up loud and hung her head out the window. She stayed in her bikini, singing along to every song that came through the car's speakers, looking good enough to eat in her tiny bikini made more obvious against my black leather seats. Savy let go. Savy was free, like I'd told she could be. Free…right up until we drove through the gates of our neighborhood.

The moment the gates closed, shutters came down over her eyes, the light all but leaving them. She reached forward and turned down the volume on the song she'd proclaimed one of her favorites. She sat up straighter and slid her sun dress over her head, straightening it until it covered her swimsuit completely. By the time I parked in my driveway her hair was braided neatly down one shoulder and she had a bottle of water in her hands. The fun-loving Savy was gone, as if she'd never existed at all. In place of the smiling, wild girl I'd witnessed minutes before, was a silent, contemplative photocopy. Not nearly as sharp and vibrant as the original.

I sighed as I turned off the ignition. "I think I like the other Savy better."

"You know what?" She turned to me, a small sad smile on her perfect pink lips. "I think I do too."

"Do you want to go to a concert tomorrow night?" I hadn't intended to invite her out again so soon. The temptation to be with her, even if it was only to be her "guide" was proving to be too great. I'd spoken without thought, without any reservations. I wanted to see her light again. I wanted to be the one to put that spark back into her sweet little soul.

She nodded, fingering the cap on her water bottle. "Yeah."

"Good. I'll pick you up at six."

She threw me a wave before she made her way across the yard separating our houses, trudging through the perfect grass her dad took care of meticulously. He tended our yard too, taking over after my dad died to help out my mom.

Savy's parents were kind people, and I guess in a way her whole family looked after mine. But the price Savy paid was much steeper than her folks.

I sat in my car long after she'd gone inside. The sun was scorching, beating through my windshield, the leather heating under my skin. A small slice of hell.

Maybe that was the punishment I deserved for wanting the only friend my brother had.

Chapter Six

Savy

Today was one of the best days of my life. I'd never felt so alive. I'd never felt so real. I was around people without having Nate hanging over me like a rain cloud about to burst open and drown everyone around him. I didn't have to worry that he was going to stare anyone down who got too close to us. I didn't have to worry about him getting into fights. Today, people talked to me and they laughed with me like I was one of them. Hanging on a summer Sunday by the lake. I wasn't wrapped in caution tape, and it felt amazing. I danced, with other kids my age. Guys held me while we moved, touching all the skin my bikini bared, exactly like all the other people dancing together.

Jeremy had given me something Nate took away. Or, more accurately, something I allowed him to take away—permission to be a whole version of myself.

I wanted more.

I rode the high of my afternoon with Jeremy all the way until I got out of the shower and found Nate lying on my bed. It was as if all my newfound energy evaporated with the steam I'd let out when I opened the door.

"Hey." It wasn't unusual for him to make himself at home in my room. He didn't knock, and my parents never stopped him. I wasn't unhappy to see him. Not at all. Guilty, maybe. Or more like Nate being here was my reality and driving with the windows down in Jeremy's car was my fantasy.

"You're sunburned." His eyes studied my pink nose and cheeks, missing nothing when it came to me, a frown on his full lips.

"Yeah, I laid out this afternoon and fell asleep." That was a bold-faced lie and it came out incredibly easy. Who was this girl I was becoming? I'd never lied to Nathan before, I'd never done anything that warranted a lie. I was always right next to him, keeping him company and keeping him in line. "How was work?"

"It was fine." He scooted over on my bed, making room for me to lay down on the soft pink blanket. "What's in the queue for tonight?"

"We could finally start season three of *Penny Dreadful*." I turned off the lamp on my nightstand and grabbed the remote before snuggling under the covers next to Nate. I rested my head on his chest, breathing in his familiar woodsy scent. I'd done this a dozen times or more, yet I wondered if these casual touches were what I wanted, or had it been going on for so long I'd been conditioned to accept this as normal.

Guilt gnawed at my insides, making my chest physically ache. I'd been complaining about my best friend, then came home and lied to his face. I was sneaking around, spending time with his older brother like a sailor on shore leave. Nate didn't deserve this from me, or from his brother. His hand rested on my hip, his lips pressing a kiss to the top of my head. He felt like home, like comfort. Like a quilt that had been washed a thousand times.

"I thought you couldn't bear to see it end?" Nate poked my ribs playfully. "We've had Josh Hartnett on ice for over a year. What gives?"

My sad small was for myself, my face still turned to the television. "All good things must come to an end, right?"

He hummed in agreement and pressed play. I wiped at the lone tear that rolled down my cheek before he could notice. I wasn't sure which ending was making me emotional, but I suddenly felt completely overwhelmed.

We watched two episodes, then Nate kissed my temple and headed home. Temple, cheek, hand. Nothing more. Ever. But still, it wasn't...normal.

I'd barely paid attention to the plot of season three. I'd spent the two hours going over my relationship with the Deacon boys with a fine-tooth comb.

I liked my quiet time with my best friend. I really did. The problem was I didn't need that quiet time to be constant and presumed. Demanded even. I rolled over onto my back and stared at my ceiling. It was still covered in glow in the dark plastic stars Nate had put up for me when we were nine. They were actual constellations. Not the usual ones like the Big Dipper either. They were less known ones like Lyra and Cygnus.

I shouldn't complain about him. He was so good to me. So caring and protective. I should consider myself lucky. I should count Nate as a blessing, not a burden.

What was wrong with me lately? Why was I being so dramatic?

Maybe it was college looming. Maybe it was the thought of living without his constant presence.

My cell vibrated on my nightstand and I reached for it presuming it was Nate telling me good night.

Stop feeling guilty for having fun today.

Jeremy. I huffed out a laugh as I sent back my reply.

How do you know I'm feeling guilty?

I can hear your conflicted thoughts all the way over here.

I did have fun.

I know you did. And you're going to have fun tomorrow too. Stop worrying about Nate. He got his Savy injection. He's fine.

Savy injection?

You're his drug, his medication. I know he ran to you as soon as he got home from work.

It's what we do.

No, it's what he needs.

I can be both people. I can be steady for him and wild for you.

You want to be wild for me, Savy?

My cheeks heated as I read his text. With. I should have used *with* instead of *for*. I'd meant *with*. Right?

I closed my eyes and remembered the feeling of being in the water with Jeremy. Of the wind in my hair and the sun on my face. It'd felt good, every single second of it. I wanted to be both. I wanted to be Nate's best friend and Jeremy's...whatever I was. I wanted to have it all, if only for a little while. I wanted the best of both worlds. Guilt be damned.

Yes.

I put my phone faced down on my nightstand, switching it to silent. I didn't want to see Jeremy's response to my bold answer. I didn't want to obsess about it if he didn't reply.

Jeremy wasn't even what this was about, not really. This was about me having some fun and finding out who I was without Nate. I needed to know *me*. Jeremy was doing me a favor, a favor that could get him in a lot of trouble with his brother. I saw the way Jeremy looked at me today. I knew he appreciated what he saw. But in two months he would be back at school and I'd be a distant memory of a summer between his sophomore and junior year of college.

Chapter Seven

Jeremy

I hadn't seen Savy in about twenty-four hours. I'd let her and my brother run alone this morning. I was being chicken shit. I was too afraid that Nathan would see the lust and need in my eyes when I looked Savannah. Last night's text was a mistake. I should've never asked her that.

You want to be wild for me, Savy?

I knew what she meant. I knew that she'd mixed up her words. But holy hell, I'd been turned on, and was breathing hard with heated skin. My pulse had started to race and it took everything in me not to crawl through her window and dare her to show me exactly how wild she could be.

Instead I'd turned my phone off to toss and turn all night. She could be wild, but she *couldn't* be wild for me. That was a line I wouldn't cross. I wouldn't do that to my brother or to her. I refused to be her first heartbreak, and that was the only way this "thing" between us could end.

"Where you headed tonight?"

Nathan stood in the hall outside the bathroom, watching me fix my hair. It could be the guilt talking, but his question sounded more like an accusation. "Concert. You wanna come?" I knew he had to work tonight, and I knew he wouldn't blow it off. It wasn't who he was. Schedules were important to him. He needed routine.

"Can't." He took a step back and leaned against the wall. "Who you going with?"

"Max and a couple of other guys from my class." I rolled up the sleeves of my white button down and headed back into my room, trying to keep my tone even and not sound like a lying bastard.

Nathan followed me. "When you leaving?"

About ten minutes after you do, bro.

"In a few." I reached into my closet and grabbed my well-loved black chucks, slipping them on. Nathan never gave two shits what I was doing or who I was doing it with. The only person's whereabouts that mattered to him were Savy's, which was exactly why the inquisition was making me feel twitchy as hell.

I didn't know what she'd told him she was doing tonight, or if she'd even bothered with a fabricated story. Maybe he assumed she'd be safely tucked into her bed since he'd be at work. Savy didn't have other friends. She didn't hang out with the girls or have date nights. I wondered if Nathan even realized she existed without him. Perhaps he thought he brought her to life when he was with her. Like a wind-up doll. "What's with all the questions?"

"Just curious." He glanced out my bedroom window, which was a direct shot into Savy's house. I couldn't see into her bedroom though. Believe me, after her cheeky wild comment last night, I'd checked. Yep. Go ahead and judge. I was pathetic.

"You sure you don't want to come? Blow off work and have some fun?" I swallowed past the lump in my throat.

"No thanks." He studied me for another few seconds and then walked off like the last five minutes of interrogation questions never even happened. I let out a sigh of relief when I heard the front door open and close.

I'd forgotten the way Nathan communicated with most people. I think the only person he ever gave the curtesy of an actual goodbye was Savy. She was different, and that had started from the moment they'd met. My dad used to call her angel baby. I thought it was because she had tons of light-covered hair and her little cheeks would get red when she laughed. But as we got older and my dad wasn't around to take care of Nathan, I saw the hidden meaning behind the nickname. She was Nathan's guardian angel.

I laid back on my bed, and took a couple steadying breathes before grabbing my cell.

Ready, wild one?

Wild One suited her better than Angel Baby. She wasn't a kid anymore. She didn't need to guard me, and she sure as hell didn't need to be good for my sake.

More than.

Meet me out front.

I bounded down the stairs and out the front door, calling bye to my mom on the way. I was excited to see Savy. Giddy even. It'd been a whole day and I was suddenly salivating at the thought of being near her again. I paused at my car door when I heard her front door click closed, the sound so familiar to me. She skipped across the green grass, her hair bouncing behind her. She wasn't wearing a stitch of makeup, and was the prettiest girl I'd ever seen.

"Good evening, gorgeous."

She blushed at my words. "Hey." She tucked her hair behind her ear and took a few timid steps in my direction.

I rounded the front of the car, opening her door before she could even reach for it. She climbed in smiling shyly. I clenched and unclenched my fists while I got in the driver's seat. Savy looked good, her smile was sweet and I wanted to kiss her lips so bad. She was the most innocent temptation I'd ever laid eyes on, and she didn't even know it.

"We're going to go pick up my friend Max and then we'll head into the city. The band we're seeing is playing at a dive bar downtown." I put the car in reverse and backed out of my driveway, my hand on the back of her seat, my fingers inadvertently brushing her silky hair.

"Oh, uh, I don't have a fake ID or anything."

I glanced over to the passenger seat as I threw the car into drive. Savy was wearing tiny cut off blue jeans shorts and a flowy bohemian looking tank top. Her long legs were crossed and the ankle boots she was rocking were perfect. Her blonde hair was wavy and once again blowing in the wind. She was a sight to behold, and any man would be absolute putty in her bashful hands.

"I don't think we'll have any trouble getting you in. No worries, okay?" She bit her lip as she nodded, and I thanked god that I was driving and had to look at the road. I reached forward and turned the radio up. "This is the band playing tonight. I've seen them a couple of times in Boston." They were a small band, mostly played college towns but they were good and always drew a fun crowd. That's what

I wanted for Savy tonight. I wanted to see her have fun. I wanted her to let loose again, to dance and laugh. To not worry about anyone but herself. She was no one's keeper when she was with me.

When I stopped outside Max's house, I threw my arm over the back of Savy's seat once again, ducking to look out her window at his front porch.

This time I touched her hair on purpose, rubbing the soft strands between my fingers. I glanced down at her lap, her hands were fidgeting, twisting the bottom of her top. I bought my palm to the nap of her neck, touching her like that was a dangerous game, but in the moment I couldn't seem to care.

"Hey, you okay?"

She nodded, biting her lip and not making eye contact with me. "Yeah, I'm good." She studied Max's house, wincing. "He's not, uh, going to say anything to Nate is he?"

I squeezed her neck gently. "Look at me, Savy." I waited until her gaze met mine before smiling. "I'm not going to let anything bad happen here, okay?" She nodded again and I used my thumb to caress her jawline. "Max won't say anything to anyone, and no one else from around here has even heard of this band. Plus, it's a twenty-one and up venue. Not many kids you and Nathan go to school with could even get in."

"It's so silly, isn't it? We're allowed to be friends, aren't we? I'm my own person. I can choose who I spend time with. I shouldn't even feel like I have to hide anything," She licked her bottom lip.

My thumb followed her tongue's path. I really hadn't meant to do that, but when I felt her small gasp I realized it'd been worth it. I was touching her too much, and too casually. I knew I was toeing a dangerous line, but I couldn't seem to make myself stop, and she didn't tell me to.

"We can spend time together, there is nothing bad happening here. You aren't doing anything wrong." I wanted her to feel safe, I wanted her to *feel*. Period. I wanted any and every reaction she'd give me. I wanted to see her happy and see her turned on. I wanted to see her wild and rebellious. I wanted to see all of her.

***

The small rundown bar was packed. Standing room only. We'd had no problems getting Savy in, they hadn't even asked to see her driver's license. Which was a miracle because she'd seemed so nervous talking to the bouncer you'd think she was smuggling coke in her tiny shorts. Speaking of her cut offs, I'd caught Max staring at her ass more times than I could count. One more and I was going to start backhanding him in the nuts.

The three of us were standing off to the side of the stage, drinks in hand. I'd gotten Savy a beer that she was nursing. Max was driving us home. He had an early session with his off-season trainer in the morning. I'd keep my count at one or two. Too many and no doubt, I'd end up trying to stick my tongue down Savy's throat.

"They're really good," she shouted next to my ear, making sure I would hear her over the music.

I put my palm on her lower back, which wasn't flirting, it was proper speaking over loud noises etiquette. "I'm glad you like them." I pointed in the direction of the stage with my drink still in hand. "You should go dance." There was a group of people that were dancing right in front of the stage. I knew she wanted to. She'd been wiggling and shaking next to me for the last thirty minutes. It was like she couldn't help but move to the beat.

She pulled her bottom lip through her teeth, torturing me. "Will you come?"

I wasn't going with her. Hell to the no. I'd seen her dance at the lake yesterday, and it was hot. By hot I meant tempting as fuck. "I'll watch you from here, I promise I won't let anyone hurt you."

She shifted on her feet, unsure of what to do. We both knew she wanted to dance, it was whether or not she was going to let go and do it. I stayed still and quiet, watching her try to decide. Then suddenly she was gone, her mind made up in an instant, and I was staring at her ass as she walked away.

I smiled so big it felt like my face was going to crack. *Good girl, Savy.*

"Stop grinning like that. You look deranged." Max elbowed me in the ribs.

I took a pull off my beer bottle. "She's dancing, man."

He shrugged. "So? Chicks dance."

"She's out there, doing exactly what she wants to do. She made up her own mind. She walked away from her comfort zone to do what *she* wanted to do." I couldn't take my eyes off her. The way her body moved, the look of pure joy on her beautiful face. She was utterly stunning in every single way that mattered. "Don't you get how great that is?"

"No. Not at all." Max cocked his head to the side, bending slightly at the knees. I flicked the crotch of his pants. "Ow, what the fuck? I was trying to see what was so miraculous about her dancing out there on her own."

"You were looking at her ass. Again." I took another drink of my beer. "What's so *miraculous* is that she's doing what she wants to do without giving a shit what anyone else thinks. That girl has spent her life taking care of my brother. Doing what was best for him. She's never left his side, has never been wild. She's never broken a law or missed curfew. She's never partied. She's never—"

"Been kissed? Been touched?" Max crossed his arms, studying me. "Is that where this is going? Is that part of it? I get that you feel guilty and want to help her live a little. I do. But it seems like you're starting to walk a very thin line."

"That's not where this is headed." I kept my eyes on Savy while I finished off my first beer. She was beginning to draw a crowd of guys. She was dancing all alone, her eyes were closed as she moved to the music. I told her I'd watch out for her, and it seemed that she trusted me completely. "I'm not walking a thin line. I'm—"

Max snorted. "You are too." He pointed out to the dance floor, to her. "That's your little brother's whole world out there. Maybe she didn't ask for the title, maybe she doesn't even want it. It doesn't matter. It's all fun games right now, man. But what happens when you end up touching her? And don't even try and tell me it's not like that because it is. I can see it in her face, and more importantly I can see it in yours."

I shook my head, denying his accusations. "I wouldn't hurt her, and I wouldn't hurt my brother."

Some hipster with a beard and suspenders wrapped his arms around Savy's waist. I took a step forward and Max shot his hand out to stop me. "Whoa, where you going?"

I gestured with my bottle. "That guy is—"

"Dancing with Savy." Max pointed out. "She looks fine with it."

He was right. Savy was smiling, moving with the stranger to the beat of a fast-paced song. She didn't appear scared. She didn't look like she needed me to step in and save her like I'd been primed to do.

Max hung his head, laughing. "You're going to get yourself in trouble with that one, Jeremy. She's not for you, man. She's Nathan's girl."

I clenched my teeth together. She wasn't Nathan's girl. She didn't want to be. She wanted to be her own girl. She wanted to be free. When I came home this summer, I saw immediately, she was drowning. She'd been treading water for too long, and was going under.

We were all to blame. My mom, her parents, me...we'd been sunbathing on the shore while she slowly sunk under the surface.

I didn't correct Max. Instead I glared daggers at the random guy who was touching her.

My fingers tightened into a fist, the beer in my hand close to shattering in my attempt to keep my cool.

I was already in trouble.

Chapter Eight

Savy

I smiled at Max, standing on my tiptoes to give him a quick peck on his cheek. He'd made me laugh that whole way home. He was a good guy and I was happy I'd gotten to know him. "Goodnight, Max. Thank you for driving us."

He stepped back, waving before he took off walking the few blocks to his house. I'd had more than two beers, and so had Jeremy. Max drove us to our street and was selflessly heading home on foot. "I feel awful that he has to walk home. I should have offered him my bike." I watched him disappear into the darkness between streetlights.

"He's fine, Savy." The two of us were standing in the shadows of our houses, the patch of grass where no light penetrated, where no one could see us. "Besides, I doubt he's walking all the way home. He usually hooks up with Mandy when he's in town, and she lives the next street over."

"Really? Mandy Blane?" I shifted on my feet. "They aren't dating? They only hang out when he's home?"

He smirked. "Yeah. You know, it's, uh, casual."

"Like friends with benefits?" I'd never had one, but I watched plenty of movies, and read plenty of books. I understood the term, and I understood its appeal too. Although I'd never admitted that out loud to anyone.

He nodded. "Yep. Exactly."

I'd never been casual with a guy, mainly because I'd never been with a guy at all. Nate and I cuddled when we watched movies and he held my hand and kissed my forehead. But I never felt anything when he did those things. No desire, no passion, no yearning for more.

After freshman year when that one brave soul had gotten his butt kicked, no one else dared to ask me out, never mind touch me. I was suddenly envious of Max, and Mandy, and anyone else that got to do what they wanted with their bodies.

"I think I'd like one of those." I clamped my lips shut after the words tumbled out. It had to be the beer talking. This was not a conversation I planned on having with anyone, let alone the constantly cool Jeremy Deacon.

"One of what?" Jeremy's brow was furrowed, his gaze on mine. The only reason I could see his face in the dark was because we were standing close, whispering. Neither one of us said it out loud, but both of us were being careful not to get caught together.

"Um, well, a friend with benefits. It seems like a nice arrangement and—"

"No."

I jerked back at Jeremy's clipped tone, embarrassed and confused as to why he'd shut me down like that. My confusion beat out my embarrassment, instead of shutting down I demanded an answer for his reaction. "It's part of growing up isn't it? It's part of learning, and it's part of life. I want to be kissed. More importantly I want to *want* to be kissed. I can't go to college this way. They'll eat me alive. I'll have my heart broken before Thanksgiving."

I was right. I knew I was. Hooking up was part of growing up, no matter how sheltered I'd been. I needed to experience it all. I *wanted* to experience it all. I felt like a bird that had been let out of her cage, and I'd be damned if I let myself get locked back up without seeing the world.

Jeremy scoffed. "What are you going to do? Hold auditions?" He was suddenly gesturing with his hands a lot, something I'd never really seen him do before. "You don't even really know any of the guys you went to school with."

I shrugged. "I don't know. Maybe Max would help me? Two casual things are better than one right?" I was mostly joking, but Jeremy definitely wasn't laughing.

"Max?" His jaw dropped open and his hands flew into the air again. "Are you high?"

Well that was rude.

"Why are you getting so upset about this?" It's not like Jeremy wanted me for himself. He wouldn't even dance with me tonight. Every time another guy came up to spin me around the dance floor I thought Jeremy would cut in, but he never did. Anyway, Max was cute, and kind. Plus, he apparently had lots of experience in the casual hook-up department.

Jeremy stepped closer, if that was even possible, his spicy scent enveloping me and making my mouth water. Why did he have to be so cute, so cool, and so yummy?

"I don't want you to get hurt, Savy. When sex comes into the picture, emotions get involved and people get hurt."

I narrowed my eyes. "Isn't that the point of a casual hook-up? To *not* let emotions get involved, to not get hurt? It's not like I'm going to fall in love the second someone puts their hand up my skirt."

"Don't talk like that." Jeremy ran his fingers through his perfect hair, making it all stand up straight.

"Like what? What is wrong with you?" I reached up and smoothed his hair into place. "You're acting like my dad."

He chuckled, the sound holding little humor. "I'm really not."

I threw my arms wide, exasperated. "What would you call it? I can't hook up with anyone, and I can't talk about someone getting into my panties. Nate? Would you rather me say you're acting like Nate? Because that one fits too."

He hung his head, his hands on his hips. "That's probably closer to the mark."

I was still buzzed from the beer, from the high of the loud music and the crowded dance floor. That had to be why I was being so open, so honest about what I wanted. Why I was touching him. I put my hands on his cheeks, picking his head up so I could look into his eyes.

"I want to live, Jeremy. I want to roll four years of high school into the next two months. This was your idea. Now that we've started, I don't want to stop. I've never felt so alive as I have with you in the last few days. The lake, the dancing, the music. You can't ask me to give it all up now."

"I'm not asking you to give it all up. If I was, I hope that you would tell me to fuck off. Not beg me to let you keep your freedom, to keep your life. It's yours and only yours." He put his hands on mine. "I don't want to see you hurt, that's all."

I dropped my hands when he dropped his. "So help me learn how not to."

***

We'd said good night an hour ago. Now I was lying in bed, staring at the stars on my ceiling. I'd barely thought about Nate all night. He'd gotten home from work about thirty minutes ago. I'd seen the lights from his car as he pulled into his driveway. When my phone vibrated on my nightstand I'd known it would be him.

You in bed?

Yep. Jammies and teeth brushed. You just get home?

Yeah. What'd you do tonight?

I sighed into my darkened bedroom, knowing that never in a million years could I tell him that I'd gone to a bar with Max and Jeremy. I could never tell him that I'd danced with strangers and drank beer. I couldn't tell him that it'd been wonderful and freeing, and that I was slowly becoming addicted to every aspect of my secret life with Jeremy. I hated lying, but I didn't have another choice, not when it came to Nate.

Netflix binge for one.

You didn't watch Penny Dreadful without me did you?

Of course not.

That's my good girl.

That's how he saw me. That's how everyone saw me. I was Nate's best friend. Which made me a *really* good girl. I didn't talk back. I didn't make waves. I was a people pleaser, and the world had no idea how many times I'd saved its ass. How many times Nate's good girl had stopped him from being really bad. I was exhausted, and overdue for a vacation.

Sorry I've had to work so much lately. I have tomorrow night off, want to do something?

Sure, that sounds fun.

Having a movie marathon in my bed with Nate didn't sound fun. It sounded comfortable and safe, but not fun. Lake parties and indie bands, now that was fun.

'Night, Sav.

Sweet dreams, Nate.

I'd spent the last thirty minutes feeling equal parts guilty for lying to Nate and giddy about all the adventures I'd had with Jeremy.

I wanted Jeremy. I'd be kidding myself to say otherwise. I understood that I was nothing more than a kid in his eyes. A summer project born out of guilt to pass the time. Sure, he flirted every once in a while. Sure, I caught a glimpse of lust in his gaze a couple of times. But that was all so fleeting.

He felt responsible for my life, or lack thereof. He was simply trying to make things right. I turned on my side, about to finally close my eyes when I noticed my phone light up again. My stomach flipped. It was probably Nate suggesting a movie for tomorrow, even though a small part of me wanted it to be Jeremy, and that small part was making big butterflies beat their wings against the walls of my stomach.

I'm sorry about earlier tonight. I had no right to tell you what to do or to say.

Jeremy. I was equal parts shocked and elated he texted me.

It's okay.

No. It isn't. Not at all. I'm not Nathan. I'm not here to tell you what you can and can't do. If you want a casual hook-up then I'll help you.

Really? Thank you.

We'll start tomorrow.

Nate wants to watch movies tomorrow night. I told him I would.

We'll head down to the lake in the morning, go for a run.

Okay.

Jeremy was going to help me find a guy to hook up with. Would that be weird? I mean, would we like make them submit references and headshots? I felt like a hook-up needed to be a little more organic than that, but hey, what the hell did I know? I'd never had a date.

Did hook-ups date? Probably not. Then it would be dating, not hooking up. My mind was racing, because I was feeling nervous. What if the hook-up Jeremy found for me wanted to start right away? Then I'd been snuggled up with Nate after making out with some random dude. That seemed wrong. But why? Nate wasn't my boyfriend.

I buried my face in my pillow and let out a little scream.

Life was a hell of a lot more complicated when you were actually living it.

Chapter Nine

Jeremy

Savy looked hot as hell in her tiny spandex running shorts and her racer back tank top. Her long blonde hair was pulled back into a sleek ponytail and she was wearing a hot pink sports bra. She was a good runner. Her strides were long and her stance was relaxed. I could've gone past her, pushed myself harder and actually got some training in, but I was more than content to stay right by her side. We rounded a sharp turn and headed down the rocky hillside. We were almost through the trees and back at the water where we started. Nathan was working the morning shift, so I only had 'til about noon with her. Not great, but necessary. Too much time alone together wouldn't be good for either of us.

"It's so hot out here." When we came to the flat land beside the lake Savy stopped with her hands on her hips. "I'm used to running before the sun comes all the way up. This is intense."

Her body was covered in sweat and her face was red. I grabbed two waters from the cooler in my car, tossing her one. "The heat's good, gets you to sweat out all those toxins."

She laughed. "The toxins from the three beers I had last night? If you're going to keep dragging me out here for runs, I'm going to start drinking more alcohol." She drained most of her water and then poured the rest down her shirt making the thin fabric stick to her body. I wanted her sports bra to spontaneously snap in two and fall to the ground.

I licked my lips. "You ready to get started?"

Savy looked around the lake, glanced over her shoulder, and then looked at me with a confused expression. "Uh, sure. Where are we going to hold auditions?"

"Auditions for what?" Maybe the heat really was too much for her.

"For my hook-up guy."

I let out a quick chuckle. "You thought we came out here to hold auditions so that I could find a guy for you to have a casual fling with?" I cocked my head to the side and narrowed my eyes. She couldn't be serious, could she? I texted her last night and I thought she—

"Yeah." She studied the wilderness surrounding us. "I wondered how you were going to get a group of guys together so early in the morning though."

I shook my head. "There are no other guys here, Savy."

"Okay, well, where are they?" She pulled her wet shirt away from her chest, using it to fan herself.

"There are no other guys, period." I finished the rest of my water, trying my best to hide my laughter. She was so sweet, and so damn innocent. For sure, I was going to hell for all the ways I was about to corrupt her.

"You said you'd help me." She threw her arms in the air, letting them fall to slap her toned thighs.

"I did, and I will." I tossed my empty water bottle in the open back window of my car.

I'd lain awake last night going over Savy's request in my head. The thought of her with another dude pissed me the fuck off. It made me want to punch a hole in the wall. That wasn't who I was, though. I wasn't reactive like that. Those genetics went to Nathan. But there was something about her that made me feel a little out of control.

The thought of her getting hurt, getting taken advantage of? No. There was no way I'd ever let something like that happen to her. It'd be like leading a lamb to slaughter. She was too good, too innocent, too pure. I barely trusted myself around her. I sure as hell didn't trust anyone else. Certainly not anyone I knew, and absolutely not anyone she went to school with. The only other person on this planet I'd trust to keep Savy safe was my brother. She didn't want him, not that way.

"You want a casual fling. I'll hook up with you."

I was going to end up the one hurt, the one used and then tossed aside. But I'd do it for her. I'd do anything for her. I'd spent the majority of my life with this girl on the outskirts of my world. I knew she existed, and I knew she played a major role in my brother's life, in keeping him sane and out of trouble. I was more than happy to let her play it too. Savy being around meant I didn't have to be the one to call him back from the edge of darkness and I could live my life the way I pleased. She was always there, always in the background standing next to Nathan. I couldn't explain it, but the second she came to stand by me, I was a goner.

"Jeremy..." She took two steps back, her tone wary.

I took two steps forward. "I don't want you to get hurt, emotionally or physically. I can't trust that to anyone else." I reached out and took her hand in mine, threading our fingers together. She didn't try to pull away, and that made me smile.

She shook her head. "If Nate ever found out it would crush him."

"What do you think would hurt Nathan more? Some asshole taking advantage of you, hurting you and using you, or him finding out that we had a little summer fling when we were kids? Think of the other guy. Even if he didn't hurt you, even if you stayed friends, if Nathan found out, he'd kill him."

I wasn't wrong, and I wasn't exaggerating, I could tell by her expression she knew it was true.

Nathan wouldn't hurt me. I was his brother. The worst he'd do was ice me out. This brilliant idea, hooking up with Savy, was literally the stupidest thing I'd do. Ever. Said the guy who had a tattoo of a swallow two inches above his dick.

There was no way I'd let her do this with anyone else, so...there was no backtracking. She wanted this, and I was going to give it to her. Figuratively give it to her, I mean.

"I don't want a pity fuck."

I jerked back like she'd slapped me, surprised she thought that of me and her casual use of the word *fuck*. "Number one, I don't pity you. I feel for you. I empathize with you. Number two, I never once said I was going to fuck you." I wouldn't do that to her. I'd decided the limits of our "fling" about two minutes after I'd decided to be her "hook-up." For Savy, having full-on sex should be something special. I'd never take that opportunity from her. It needed to go to someone she loved, someone she wanted a life with. We had no future. When the summer ended and we went our separate ways, we'd be over. It wasn't ideal, but it was a compromise I'd force myself to live with. For her. When this summer was no more than a faded memory for Savy, I'd still have a scar on my heart since we could never be anything more. "Either you take what I'm offering, or you can go find someone else. Alone. I won't be a part of you getting hurt."

She pulled her lower lip through her teeth, her eyes on where our hands were connected. "I don't want you to, um, I just, uh, I don't want you to do something you don't want to. Okay? I know I'm not your type, and I know I'm just a kid in your eyes and—"

I pulled her to me, snaking my hand behind her neck, and put my lips on hers. I let go of her hand and put my palm right above her perfect toned ass. I pressed her body against mine, letting her feel exactly how much she was so my type I couldn't've conjured up anyone better.

After a few long moments holding her to me, I pulled back slightly, keeping her body right where it was. "Savy, you are gorgeous. You are funny and you're smart. You have a wild streak in you about a mile wide that's begging to be let loose, baby. I want you. Even though I shouldn't, even though it's wrong. I want to touch you, kiss you, fucking taste you. Don't ever for a second think that this is me doing you a favor. This is me doing myself one."

"So you're really going to be my fling?" Her question was spoken in a soft whisper.

I nodded. "Two months. You and I doing whatever you want to do for the next sixty days. Then I leave for school, and so do you and Nathan." We had an end date. We'd go into this knowing it wasn't forever. I told myself it would make it all so much easier. Yeah. Like I believed that. "You game?" This was the stupidest, most dangerous thing I'd done in my entire life. Yet, I was fucking pumped.

"Yes." She answered me without hesitation, her response like air across my lips.

I fused my mouth back to hers, my hands on her jaw. I nipped at her lower lip that she loved to bite so much. I used her tiny gasp of shock to my advantage, slipping my tongue in her mouth. I angled her head back, towering over her and taking our kiss deeper. Her hands fisted in my shirt, pulling me closer.

"Tell me how far you want to go today, wild one?" I needed to know my limit, because the longer I kissed her, the more I wanted. She might be new at this, but kissing her...it was the best kiss of my life.

"Keep kissing me, please."

I walked her backward, into the cool shade of the woods. It was hot outside, and getting hotter by the second. I pushed her against a large tree and then started devouring her. This time I let my hands roam all over her tight body. I touched every strip of skin I could find. I would've gladly spent the rest of my day sweating in this sun if it meant I got to keep kissing Savy. I wanted more, I wanted to taste all of her. I wanted her naked in the water. I wanted—"

"Crap. Hold on, My cell keeps going off." She pulled her phone out of the band of her shorts. "It's Nate. He's called five times."

I rested my forehead against hers, panting. From being turned on, and from the restraint of not taking this make out session any further. "You should answer."

Or you should throw your cell in the lake.

Her gaze darted to mine as she slowly brought her phone to her ear. "Hey, Nate. What's up?"

My hand shot out, grabbing her cell and putting it on speaker phone. I wasn't sure why, but suddenly I was irritated at the thought of them sharing a conversation I wasn't part of. My tongue had been in her mouth seconds ago. Surely, this possessive feeling would subside...eventually. She shot me a funny look, but didn't switch it back.

"What are you doing? Why are you so out of breath?" My brother sounded concerned, not jealous. Which made me feel like an ass, but didn't stop me from smiling. I'd made her breathless. I dipped down and placed a kiss on her collarbone and her head fell back against the tree trunk with a soft thunk.

"I just got back from a run." She licked her lips and I held her wrist, pushing her hand and the phone farther away from us. I kissed her. I couldn't help it. She put her free hand on my lower back and pulled my pelvis against hers. I whispered, "Do what feels good, wild one," against the shell of her ear. She was a quick study.

"You went for a run alone?" *Typical Nathan.*

She brought her phone back to where Nathan could hear us, and I backed away. "It's daylight."

"You should've asked Jeremy to go with you. I don't like you running alone. What if you get hurt? Or what if someone tries to take you?" I raised my eyebrows in shock.

He must be really worried if he wanted *me* to go with her. His concern was ridiculous in the extreme. She was an adult running in the daylight. Of course I wouldn't want her running in the woods alone, but for all Nathan knew she was running in our neighborhood.

"Next time. But I'm home, safe and sound. No kidnapping attempts, no broken bones." She looked away from her phone and caught me staring. She smiled. I put my mouth back to her ear. *Hang up now Savy, I'm not finished kissing you.* "Is that why you called?" She was clearly irritated, but she'd never let him know it. Her tone sounded even and friendly.

"No, I called to let you know that I got the end of my shift covered. I'll be home in about an hour. Maybe we can do lunch before our movie?"

She kept her eyes on mine. I knew what she was thinking. She wanted me to tell her to tell him no. She wanted me to beg her to stay here with me a little bit longer. I wasn't going to do that. That wasn't what this was. Savy wasn't my girlfriend. She wasn't mine to keep. I wouldn't ruin my brother's life over this fling. No one would get hurt on my watch. If Savy wanted to deny my brother, she was going to have to do it on her own accord. She'd need to find that strength inside herself. Getting it from me wouldn't help her break the Nathan cycle she'd lived for years.

I stayed silent. She dipped her head, breaking our eye contact. "Yeah, Nate. That sounds great. Text me when you get home and I'll meet you outside."

"See you soon, Sav."

She hung up and let her arm fall to her side. "I guess you better get me home then." Her tone was clipped, short even. A tone I'd never heard her take with anyone else. It didn't bother me. I loved it. She could be irritated and pissed off. She could be whatever she wanted to be around me. No eggshells to walk on here.

I grabbed her hand, all but dragging her to my car. Once she was in and her seat belt was fastened I fish tailed away from the lake shore. I was speeding, and I intended to keep speeding until I pulled into my driveway.

"Why are you driving so fast? Can't wait to get rid of me?" She kept her gaze trained out the passenger side window.

I reached over and put my hand on her upper thigh, giving it a soft squeeze. "It takes fifteen minutes to get home, ten if I drive like this. Which gives us a good ten minutes to park the car, and sneak into your empty house.

"When I said I wasn't done kissing you, I meant it, baby."

Chapter Ten

Savy

He called me baby. I freaking melted. For years I'd been waiting for him to see me that way. I kept quiet and kept my hands to myself on the drive home, but I was itching to touch him, to kiss him again. I was shocked that Jeremy had decided to be my hook-up and that he actually wanted me. That I turned him on. It made me feel powerful, and it made me feel alive. Which was exactly what he wanted for me, and what I wanted for myself.

He threw the car in park and then jogged around to my door, opening it and pulling me out. We ran like two little kids, hand in hand to my house. Through the front door, up sixteen stairs and then into my bedroom. The room that I'd slept in since I was six years old when my parents bought this house. The bed on which I watched movies with Nate.

"You know, for someone who has only been kissed once in eighteen years, you're a good kisser Savannah Nightingale." Jeremy twirled me around and then backed me up against my closed bedroom door, capturing my mouth with his once again.

He kissed me until I was breathless, then he began placing pecks along the column of my throat. I laughed. "You know I have a bed. Wouldn't that be much more comfortable than this door?" I swallowed hard, trying to keep my composure while he tortured me with his mouth. This make-out session had turned my brain foggy.

"Mmmm, yes it would be." His hands grabbed my butt cheeks, pulling me tighter against him. "But if we move to the bed, if we get comfortable, I'll be tempted to take things further."

I bit my lip to keep from letting out a moan when his thumb brushed over my nipple through my shirt. Everything on my body felt so sensitive. "We can do that. We can take things further."

He shook his head, his nose brushing against my chest as he kissed lower. "We really can't. We're about out of time, and the next step is one of my favorites. To do it properly, I need to be able to go slow. To take my time."

His lips moved back to mine. He was towering over me again so he could kiss me deeper. Now I knew what lust felt like, and longing. This was what it meant to want someone. To want to be touched and tasted. The beer, the music, the dancing. The freedom. Of all the experiences Jeremy had gifted me so far, this was my favorite one.

"Sav. You up there?"

Jeremy and I both froze at the sound of Nate's voice coming from downstairs. I hadn't heard him pull in, and I hadn't heard the front door open. I was so completely consumed with Jeremy and what he was making me feel, everything else had fallen away.

I met his gaze. I was panicked, he seemed less affected but still shaken.

He put his lips to my ear and whispered. "Tell him you're changing and you'll be right down."

I turned and cracked my door enough to stick my head out. "Hey, I'm changing, I'll be down in a sec."

"Okay. Take your time, I'm going to grab a glass of water."

I shut the door, throwing the lock and then sagging against it. I picked my head up to find Jeremy at my closet, going through my clothes. "What are you doing?"

He turned to look at me over his shoulder, his hands still on my clothes. "I'm trying to find you something to wear, you don't want to keep Nathan waiting, do you?" His voiced sounded strained, like he wasn't pleased with the interruption.

I wanted to think it was because he wanted to stay, but it probably had more to do with the fact that his brother almost caught us.

"I'm not changing with you in here." I knew that part of hooking up would be him seeing me naked. But I was sweaty and gross and I wasn't ready for that moment to happen yet.

"Well, I can't leave. He'll see me. You can't go down there in your running clothes because then he'll know you lied to him." He put his hands on his hips, his eyes wide.

I grabbed the outfit he'd pulled out and made a spinning motion with my finger. "Turn around?" He did what I asked and I changed as quickly as I could. A long red and white striped t-shirt and a pair of shorts. The longest pair of shorts I owned. My grandma had bought them for me. I looked like a character in "Where's Waldo" but I didn't have time to be picky. I ran around my room, found my shoes and put on fresh deodorant. When I had my hand on the door to leave, Jeremy put his palms on my hips and pulled me back against him.

His nose ran from my neck to my ear, his soft breath sending chills down my spine. "I'll come running with you and Nathan in the morning, okay?"

I nodded. "Okay."

I went to pull the door open and he put his palm out to stop me. "Turn around, Savy." When I did, he dipped down and kissed me one last time. Stealing the air from my lungs and the sense from my brain. I sagged against him.

I didn't want to leave. I wanted more of this. I wanted to kiss him until I fell asleep from sheer exhaustion.

He moved away all too soon.

"Have fun, wild one."

***

The car ride with Nate was nothing like my rides with Jeremy. Nate was quiet, the radio turned down low. When he spoke it wasn't his voice fighting against the wind of an open window. Not that Nate was all that talkative in the first place. When we were kids, Nate once went three whole weeks without saying a single word to anyone. The only person he'd communicate with was me, using his tiny block script on a dry erase board I kept in my room.

What had finally broken his silence was me falling off my bike. I'd broken my wrist and he'd screamed for my parents. I was crying so hard he'd been afraid to pick me up and carry me home like he normally would have. After that, he started talking again like nothing had happened. No one thought to ask him why he'd stopped speaking in the first place. It was simply Nate's way.

This silence today seemed loaded. Heavy. Like there was more to it than his odd personality traits. He'd been quiet when we were seated at one of our favorite restaurants, quieter than he normally was. I was afraid he was picking up on my mood, afraid he could sense the change in me.

"Hey, you okay? You seem distracted." Nate wasn't eating his food. He was more or less pushing it around on his plate. If one of us was distracted, it should be me. I kept replaying my morning with Jeremy over and over in my head on a loop filled with elation and guilt in equal measure. My lips could still feel Jeremy's kisses, and my body heated from the memory of his hands on me.

"I'm worried about next year, about school. I don't want to be without you, Sav, I can't imagine us not being together all the time." He finally took a large bite of his burger as if getting his concerns off his chest gave him the will to eat.

I hated the uncertainty in his voice, and, as usual I had the strong urge to comfort him. It was ingrained in me, a part of who I was. Make Nate feel better, make Nate feel cared for, make Nate sane. What about Savy never crossed my mind.

"Hey, you know I love you, right?" I waited for him to nod, and he did, once. "You and I, we're family. We'll still talk all the time. We can see each other on weekends and school breaks. You know I want what's best for you, and what's best for you is Yale."

"Where *you* are is best for me." The emotion in his voice, the yearning, it made my heart hurt, and it made me feel like a jerk for sneaking around behind his back. I wasn't deceitful by nature, and lying to Nate felt wrong on so many levels. But I wouldn't give up Jeremy, and I wouldn't give up the freedom I'd experienced these last few days. Not for anything or anyone. I knew that now without a doubt. It was time for me to take a selfish, to quote another show we'd binged together over the years.

"No, what's best for you is *Yale*. What's best for me is Emerson." I smiled at him, reaching across the table and taking his hand while trying once again to reassure him that I wasn't abandoning him. "Nothing is going to change between us, no matter how far apart we live."

I was feeling stifled. I was longing for a life that wasn't run by Nate's moods and fits. I *did* love him. He'd been my best friend for as long as I could remember. I'd never cut him out, I'd never leave him to fend for himself. I wasn't deserting him. I was asking for a little space to learn who I was.

"What if I want something to change?" he said softly, but with determination. "Something between us."

I stopped breathing. Time stood utterly still and trepidation started creeping through my veins like a poison. I sent up a silent prayer to god, to the universe, to anyone who was listening. Please don't let this be happening, not after all this time. I couldn't have Nate tell me he wanted more. If he did, if he spoke those damning words out loud, my life was over.

I swallowed thickly, leaning forward forcing a small smile on my face. "What?" I pretended like I hadn't heard him. I pretended like my whole world wasn't moments away from completely shattering. I played dumb, and hoped he'd chose to let his question go.

He stared at me, his dark eyes searching my face. His hand was still holding mine across the table, his thumb moving gently back and forth across my wrist. I worked hard as hell not to let my fear show.

Eventually, he shook his head. "Nothing. It was nothing."

Quietly, I let out the breath I'd been holding, thankful to let his words float off into the atmosphere and dissolve into nothingness.

If Nate truly wanted more we were all in trouble.

I squeezed his hand. "We have two months to hang out. One last summer to enjoy being right next door to each other. Let's stop thinking about the fall and enjoy our time together, okay?" I drew in a deep inhale, trying to calm my erratic pulse. I felt like I'd dodged a bullet aimed right at my heart.

He nodded and then ate everything on his plate and what was left on mine. Nate had to go to Yale, there was no other option. I was going to Emerson.

I couldn't live the next four years the way I'd lived the last twelve.

After lunch we went to my house and climbed into my bed. Nate suggested we finish the final season of Penny Dreadful. He laid behind me, his body pressed right up against mine. Tighter than usual. There had been more than one time over the last few hours he'd brushed the hair off my neck or rubbed his hand on my stomach. It didn't feel the same as when Jeremy touched me. I didn't long for more. I didn't crave Nate's kisses.

He'd never tried to take things further, and he'd never acted like he wanted anything intimate. *Why now?* I wondered if I was doing something to make him react this way. Maybe he sensed my attention was elsewhere. I didn't think he could he tell I'd spent the whole morning lusting after someone who wasn't him. Maybe he felt an urgency to get closer since summer was all we had left before we went our separate ways. Maybe it was his fear of the unknown, of being without me next year. My brain was going in a million different directions, I couldn't even concentrate on the show we were watching.

Eventually, thankfully, he fell asleep.

I felt like I could relax for the first time since he'd quietly told he'd wanted more, and then had taken it back. Probably because of the way I reacted.

Chapter Eleven

Jeremy

I was lying in my bed, reading the *Great Gatsby*, counting down the minutes until my brother came through the front door. It was midnight now. He'd been with Savy for twelve hours. I wasn't jealous, I was worried about him smothering her. I knew she felt trapped, and I was sure being with him for that long was difficult, especially since for the first time in their long-ass friendship, she had to lie to him about how she'd been spending her time. About her day. I knew it'd hurt her to do it. She was a good person with a kind heart. She cared about my little brother. Unfortunately, she cared about him more than she cared about herself.

Hell, she'd sacrificed her life for his happiness.

After she'd gone downstairs, I'd watched her and Nathan walk to the Tahoe hand in hand. She didn't look at him the way she looked at me. She didn't want him, and I hated how tightly I held onto that.

I'd watched Nathan open her door and help her up into the truck. I watched them pull away. After they left, like a creeper I sat in Savy's room surrounded by her things, by her scent. I looked at the pictures on her walls, so many of her and Nathan, and a few of her and her parents. One snap was of all of us when we were little. It was taken before my dad passed away. We'd gone to a barbeque or something. Our parents were standing in the background and we three kids had our arms around each other. Nathan was looking at Savy and she was looking at me. I couldn't help but smile. How had I missed this?

I hung my head and made my way downstairs and outside, crossing the driveway to my house. I'd never seen Savy looking at me like that because I hadn't wanted to. Now, in retrospect, I must've known what it would mean if she wanted me. It would hurt Nathan. Chicken-shit move, I'd avoided it and ignored it. She was my kid brother's salvation and nothing more. But slowly, over time, I'd began to see her as her own person. Now...fuck. Here we were, right where we should never be.

I felt like a selfish prick. Nathan had been in some form of love with Savannah Nightingale almost his entire life. Me? I'd swooped in with a hell of a crush and the need to set her free. In three days, I'd put everything they'd built over the last thirteen years in jeopardy. I was a shit big brother, I knew that. I told myself this wasn't about me or Nathan, it was about Savy. And that girl needed me. She needed to taste freedom on the tip of her wicked little tongue. She needed to live, she needed to know what it felt like so she'd keep chasing it at all costs.

She needed to want to choose herself first and foremost, and she needed to choose for herself what she wanted and needed in her life.

My cell vibrated on my desk and I groaned. I figured at this hour it would be Max trying to get me to go out. He'd begged me to hit a party over at Mandy's cousin's lake house. I'd declined, although I wasn't really sure why. A distraction would have been perfect. He'd been peppering me with party pics of half-naked girls for the last forty-five minutes, trying like hell to entice me.

So when I saw Savy's name on the screen, I couldn't help the grin that took over my face. I didn't realize how much I'd been anticipating her reaching out. I wanted to know how her day with Nathan went. I wanted to know if she was okay.

Nate fell asleep.

I tried not to picture him in bed beside the girl I'd had my lips all over hours before. I didn't want to think about punching my younger brother out of jealousy. This situation didn't need violence added in because my dick was feeling possessive.

You want me to call and wake him up?

No, I didn't want you or your mom to worry about him not coming home.

Did she normally text my mom when Nathan stayed at her house? I doubted that. My mom knew if Nathan wasn't here, he was with Savy. She'd never demand he leave his safe space until he was good and ready. Did that mean that Savy wanted *me* to know that

Nathan was still with her? I knew she wasn't trying to make me jealous. One, that wasn't who she was. Two, she'd have no reason to assume I would be. We were friends who made out. Well, that's what I keep telling myself. I was helping her with a personal summer project. That was it. Maybe she was looking for a reason to text me, looking for a reason to reach out. That, I could understand.

He's a bed hog, but I'm used to it.

He's in your bed?

I figured he was, but it didn't mean I had to like it. He didn't need to be sleeping in her bed. What the hell was wrong with her fucking parents? She'd told me they didn't bat an eye when they'd walked into her bedroom in the morning and he was there. She'd told me they never questioned him being in her bed, never questioned if anything was going on between the two of them. I wondered if it was because they knew she didn't see Nathan as more than a friend or because either way, they would never stand between Nathan and what he needed to feel whole.

We were watching a show.

Like that was all the explanation I needed. They were so close, so comfortable together. They watched movies in her bed, snuggled together. I closed my eyes, fighting the image of my brother wrapped around Savy, breathing in her sweet scent. Did he get hard when he held her? Did he long to kiss her neck? It wasn't fair of me to feel this way. This was Nathan's life, and he'd loved her for most of it. My jealousy needed to chill the fuck out.

Pretend to be asleep.

What?

I pulled up my favorites list and tapped Nathan's name with a little more force than necessary. Apparently my jealousy had zero desire to chill. Instead it wanted to rage. The phone rang four times before he answered it in a sleepy voice. "Hello?"

"Hey, man. Where are you?" I was trying really hard to control the annoyance in my tone, the edge I was feeling.

"I'm with Sav. What do you need?" He was whispering, which meant she'd done what I told her to, she'd closed her pretty eyes and pretended to sleep.

"You, uh, you want to hit a party with me? It's down by the lake, I was thinking about going for an hour or so." I had no plans to get out of my bed and head to that party. But I'd do it if it meant getting

Nathan away from Savy. I told myself it was for her, so she could get some space.

I was lying.

He let out a quiet chuckle, the sound holding no humor. "You want me to leave Savy's nice warm bed, which she's in with me, to go to a party? Did you call the right number?"

I ground my molars together. He wasn't wrong, it was a complete long shot, a Hail Mary pass if I'd ever seen one. But I'd been compelled to make it. "Thought I'd ask, man. No big deal."

"Sav is already asleep, I'm staying here tonight. See ya in the morning." He hung up and I resisted the urge to throw my phone across the room.

Of course he wouldn't want to leave her bed.

I couldn't blame him.

The problem was, I wanted to trade places with him.

Chapter Twelve

Jeremy

I'd been up since five in the morning and had downed three cups of piping hot blacker than night coffee already. I hadn't slept well after my call with Nathan. I'd fought jealousy, and self-righteousness while I'd tossed and turned all night. When I had managed sleep, I'd been plagued with nightmares about Savy drowning in the lake and Nathan holding me hostage on the shoreline, refusing to let me save her.

It didn't take a psychologist to interpret that shit. It was the most literal nightmare in the history of nightmares. I'd tried to rescue her last night, and Nathan stood his ground.

Either way, I was wound pretty tight from the coffee, the lack of sleep, and the jumble of emotions at seeing Savy and Nathan together. They were out front, stretching in our driveway, dressed to go on a run. Where had Nathan even pulled running clothes from? Did he keep stuff at her house? Did he stay over there that often that he would? I tried to tell myself I was bothered by it for her, but my jealousy was rearing its green-eyed head too frequently to brush off at this point.

"Morning." I winced at the loud tone of my over caffeinated voice.

"Hey, Jer." Savy was smiling, but biting her lip to keep it from getting too big. She was as happy to see me and I was to see her. I hadn't missed her or anything. That would be stupid.

Nathan was stretching his legs on the bumper of his Tahoe. "Are you running with us this morning?" He glanced up at me and then back down to his stretching, like he could care less either way.

"Yeah. That cool?" I was jogging in place, bouncing on the balls of my feet to warm up.

"Sure." He switched legs. "But why in the hell are you yelling?"

I shrugged, still bouncing. "Couldn't sleep well, got up early and made some coffee."

Nathan stood straight and threw his arm around Savy, pulling her to his chest and kissing the top of her head, making her long ponytail sway with the movement. "We slept great, didn't we, Sav?"

Savy winced, and I had to work hard to school the distaste from showing on my face. He'd never done that before. He'd never felt the need to throw their connection at me like a fast ball. Maybe he had and I'd never cared until this moment. Nathan was either on to me, or he'd always been a bit of a boastful douche when it came to the girl trapped under his massive arm.

There was nothing I could say in rebuttal: no move for me to make. I chose to ignore his comments. "Great. Let's go." I took off at a faster pace than I normally used when I ran with Savy but she lengthened her stride and easily caught up with me.

"Stop being weird," she whispered so only I could hear her. Nathan was a few paces behind us. He was all bulk, he'd never be able to keep up with us.

"I'm not being weird. I told you, I've had too much coffee." I smiled brightly and slowed my stride, letting Nathan join.

I *was* being weird. She was right and the coffee hadn't helped. I woke up feeling weird. Wired, and anxious. I didn't like that Nathan spent the night in Savy's bed. I didn't like that Savy's parents allowed it. She hadn't wanted him to stay, and he never even thought to ask her what she preferred. He *never* fucking had.

I also didn't like that he'd rubbed it in my face either. I swear, I never remembered him doing that before. Though to be fair, I never really paid attention before.

I was jealous, but Nathan was selfish. Of course, I believed my "affliction" was the lesser of two evils. "What are you doing today, man? You have to work again?"

"Nah. I'm off today."

Well, fuck, that meant that I wouldn't be able to see Savy. My mood turned bleak, like a rain cloud had opened up over my head. Like I was fucking Eeyore from *Winnie the Pooh*. "Oh. Okay. Great." It wasn't that I wanted to kiss her, touch her, and feel her little body move against mine. Well. It wasn't *only* that. I also wanted to make her laugh, to make sure she had fun. I wanted her to have the type of day *she* wanted, not the type of day being with Nathan allowed. "What are your plans then?"

I could feel Savy staring at me out of the corner of her eye, and it took everything inside me not to meet her gaze. We were playing a dangerous game, like Max had predicted only days before. One wrong move could bring it all crashing to a halt. The *I told you so* shit he was going to give me was really going to chap my ass.

Nathan shrugged. "I don't know. No plans really, other than hang out with Sav."

"Great." If I said that word one more time, I might hurl. I turned to Savy, my smile most likely manic by this point. "What do you plan on doing today?"

"Uh, I don't know, maybe—"

"Let's have a party tonight." I cut her off, accidentally screaming again. I wasn't trying to be rude, but I wanted to offer her another option before she retreated into her shell and let Nathan control her whole damn day. "Mom's away visiting Aunt Karenna, and all my friends are back in town for the summer. We have the pool. I'll get a keg. It'll be fun," I was practically shouting.

I winced. *Fuck.* I needed to stop talking so damn loud. Note to self, three cups of black coffee was my limit.

Nathan made a face filled with pure disgust. "A party?"

He hated small talk and girls trying to coax him into speaking to them. He barely tolerated family dinners. Strangers were a definite no go.

Nathan hated people. He hated people invading his space and touching his things. I wondered what he would say if he knew I'd touched Savy? I gave myself a mental head shake. That was not something I needed to be thinking about right now.

"It'll be fun. What do you say, Sav? You game?"

She glanced between me and Nathan, giving him one of her persuasive smiles. The one I'd seen her use when she was trying to coax him into or out of something. "Sounds good to me. I didn't have anything else to do today." Poor girl had no doubt mastered that smile by the time she was ten. "Nate?"

He shrugged, immediately and shockingly giving into what she wanted. "Sure. Whatever."

I fist pumped the air like an overly caffeinated tool. Nathan and Savy wouldn't be spending the day holed up in her house together. A party was a good distraction. Hell, maybe Nathan would have some fun and loosen up. I chuckled, in my mind of course. The thought of Nathan ever having fun at party was actually ridiculous. But this wasn't about him, and it wasn't about me. This was about Savy and my promise to her.

My promise to set her free.

Chapter Thirteen

Savy

The music was loud, the pool was full of people, and there was a keg of beer tapped and on ice in the kitchen. Definitely a party. Jeremy'd had a few parties here and there when he was living at home, but Nate never wanted to go. I'd watched from my bedroom window, stealing glances when he wasn't looking. I'd longed to be there, surrounded by people laughing and dancing, but I'd kept my mouth shut, because that wasn't Nate's scene and I knew it'd make him uncomfortable.

I'd even watched Jeremy make out with a girl once. He pulled her off to the side, away from the chaos and picked her up. Her legs had wrapped around his waist and they'd kissed for what felt like hours. I hadn't been jealous of her, not really. I was simply envious of her freedom. She was able to make her own choices. That had been how she wanted to spend her night, and she went for it. Consequences be damned. He'd carried her around the pool and into the house, his hands never leaving her ass. I'd known what they were going to do.

After they'd disappeared, I'd climb back in bed snuggling up to Nate. I remembered feeling guilty for wanting to be at the party, for wanting to be that carefree girl. I had my best friend sleeping peacefully beside me and I should've been counting my blessings, not wishing I were someone else.

Things were changing since I'd begun learning what freedom felt like. What fun was. I'd never be that girl. I'd never be the girl Jeremy picked up in front of a crowd of people and carried to his bed. It wasn't in the cards for us. It never had been.

"You having fun, wild one?" Jeremy spoke softly against the shell of my ear, making those chills only he could conjure shoot down my spine. Nate had left my side for the first time tonight to go to the restroom, two minutes ago. It seemed like Jeremy been watching and waiting for a moment when I was alone. I hoped so. I wanted him to want me that much.

"Yep" I popped the p on the word, then turned around to face him with a small smile on my face. "I'm having a great time."

He grinned, sarcastically. "Looks like it." He put his hand on my hip and pulled my body flush against his, quickly brushing a kiss on the corner of my mouth before backing up a few steps. "You're hot as hell, Savy. Every pair of male eyes in this room are trained on that short little dress you're wearing."

I hadn't dressed for the other guys at the party, I'd chosen the pale blue sundress for Jeremy, and Jeremy only. His eyes were the ones I wanted trailing down my body, drooling over my exposed thighs. When I'd come downstairs to meet Nate at my front door, his eyes had narrowed. I could tell he didn't want me to wear something so short in front of all these people. To his credit, he'd kept his mouth shut. Although, like I said, he'd only left my side once since we'd gotten here an hour ago.

"Dance baby, you know you want to. I can see your body vibrating." Jeremy reached out and trailed a fingertip down my arm, the simple touch setting me on fire.

Baby. That word made my breath shutter in my chest. Jeremy affected me. Everything he did and said a tantalization. I'd had a crush on him since I was a kid, and it was growing in intensity with every interaction.

I wanted to dance, he was right. But that wasn't possible, not tonight. "Nate wouldn't like that. He wouldn't want me in the middle of the crowded dance floor, it'll put him on edge." No one would dare try to dance with me anyway. They all knew how Nate was, how over-protective he could be. I sighed, suddenly feeling defeated. "This is stupid, I should go home."

That would be safest for everyone. Nate would be happy as a clam. He'd follow me home and snuggle us under my covers. He'd want nothing more than for me to tell him we didn't have to stay. The only reason he was here was because I'd asked him to be. He didn't enjoy parties. He didn't enjoy crowds. Instead of getting uncomfortable and removing himself from the situation, he'd get agitated to the point of anger. It never ended well.

"Really, I'll take Nate back to my house and—"

"No." Jeremy's hand shot out, grabbing my wrist, his thumb stroking over my pulse making my insides ignite. After our intense make-out sessions, I knew the feeling Jeremy instantly invoked was lust. I understood now what happened when a crush was reciprocated. Boy, it was dangerously addicting.

"Stay and have fun." He tugged me a step closer. "What's the worst that could happen, huh? He goes and sulks in his room?" He shrugged like this conversation wasn't perilous. "You're safe. You're in a comfortable place. I'm here, and Nathan is here. There's no reason you should have to stay right next to him."

Jeremy was delusional. But. He was also right. Nathan couldn't possibly worry about my safety. We were in *his* house. If he got mad, he *could* go hang in his room for a bit. Although he probably wouldn't.

I glanced around at the crowd, envious of the good time everyone seemed to be having, Laughing, talking, dancing. I wanted to dance, I wanted to talk to the kids I'd grown up with, the ones I'd never been given the chance to know. Maybe I could set a timer on my watch and I'd hide myself amongst my peers for a while before I did everyone a favor and got Nate out of here.

Max walked up, interrupting my internal planning session when he tossed his arm around Jeremy's broad shoulders. "Hey, man. Nice party." He looked at me, grinning easily. "Hey, Savy. Where's your other half?"

Jeremy elbowed him in the ribs as I gestured with my head down the hallway. "Bathroom."

Max chuckled. "Well it only took you two eighteen years, but you got Nathan to a party."

"Yeah. Savy's magic." Jeremy stroked the pulse of my wrist again. I pulled my bottom lip between my teeth. Undeniably turned on by a guy that I couldn't ever truly have, I still couldn't help but want Jeremy to pull me into the nearest closet and kiss me senseless. His mere touch was making me crazy.

"Are you two fucking kidding me?" Max shook his head, glancing at our joined hands, laughing humorlessly. "Seriously?"

Jeremy jerked his hand back like my skin was made of hot lava. Then he grabbed Max by the back of the neck and steered him in the direction of the patio door. He glanced back at me over his shoulder and winked. I made a step to follow them and find out what Max had been talking about but Nate snaked his arms around my waist from behind startling me.

"Sorry, Sav. Didn't mean to scare you."

I turned around and looked up into his dark eyes. My small window had closed, Nate was back and I doubted he'd leave me alone again. I twisted my lips to the side, deciding to try a new direction. "I want a beer."

His eyes narrowed. "Since when?"

"Since right this instant." I nodded and took his hand in mine, pulling him into the packed kitchen. We paused in front of the keg and he filled a cup for each of us. Expertly. No foam. When had Nathan learned to do that? He didn't go to parties, and he never stayed home when Jeremy had them here. He always preferred to hide at my house until things calmed down and people left.

I took a big sip from the plastic cup he handed me, then another. Maybe I couldn't leave his side, maybe I couldn't dance, but I could drink. I could let the alcohol dull everything I couldn't have. I'd never used drugs or liquor as a crutch. I figured I was owed this one.

"Let's go outside." I went to walk off and Nate grabbed my hand, threading his fingers through mine. We looked like a couple. Not that it really mattered. No one besides Jeremy and Max were going to talk to me anyway. He let me lead him out to the back patio. The music playing from the outdoor speakers was from the band I heard the other night. The concert Jeremy took me too, or more like snuck me into. I smiled at the memory.

Nate put his arm around my neck and pulled me closer, tucking me against his side. "What has you smiling like that, Sav?"

"This song. I really love this band." I'd downloaded some of their older songs the day after I'd seen them live. I wasn't sure if I actually enjoyed their music, or if I was simply obsessed with the emotions they invoked. Their sound reminded me of freedom, of dancing and the feel of someone's hands on my hips.

"You do? I've never heard them before."

Jeremy sauntered up, knocking his cup against his little brother's in a silent, *cheers.* "Is my baby brother drinking a beer?" His eyes went wide when they landed on my cup. "Whoa. Savy's having one too. Well. I'll be damned." His smile was too bright, his voice too happy.

I'd learned over the last week that when Jeremy was trying to appear unaffected, he turned up the charm *and* the volume. To me it screamed guilt, but that might have only been because I knew what his cheerfulness was hiding. Nate, on the other hand, ignored his brother's sarcasm as Jeremy and I both started singing along to the chorus blasting through the outdoor speakers.

Jeremy glanced at me, his smile went from forced to real when his gaze met mine. I bit my lip, trying to hide what his attention was doing to me. We were lost in the memory of that night, of the crowded bar and the laughter on our way home.

"How do you both know this band? I've never heard any of these songs." Nate was looking between us, brow furrowed.

Jeremy laughed, too loud, once again. "You need to get out more little brother, this band is everywhere." He turned his cup up, draining it dry. "Anyone else need a refill?"

I did the same with mine and held it out. "Me."

Nate took my cup, even though Jeremy reached for it and was the one who offered. "I'll get it, Sav," Nate said, following his big brother back into the house, leaving me alone, which was far from the norm. I was thankful for the small reprieve. As I let out a deep breath, I tipped my head back to see the night sky.

One smile from Jeremy was all it took to make me feel all antsy and fidgety. I wanted him to touch me. I wanted him to pull me into a dark corner and put his hands on me again. It'd been too long. I was hooked, craving his lips like an addict.

"Hey, Savannah, right?"

I picked my head up, a boy from my senior Lit class was standing in front of me, making eye contact. I'd seen him at the lake last weekend, we'd danced for a bit before Jeremy had told me it was time to go home. He'd been nice, kind even.

"Yeah." I closed one eye, wincing and trying to remember his name. "Keaton?"

He nodded and held his hand out for me to shake. "It's nice to see you again."

I put my hand in his, squeezing lightly. "You too." He didn't let go of my hand and I started to giggle when his smile stayed in place.

He was into me. This handsome normal guy was actually into me. Flirting with me at a party. How different my life would have been if I'd been able to be a normal teenager. Been able to party, have fun, and flirt with boys.

"So, where are you headed in the fall?" He finally let go of my palm.

"Emerson. You?"

"My dad lives down in Louisiana, my grandparents too. I'm going to live with him and go to LSU." He reached out and brushed a lock of hair off my forehead. "Have you ever been down south?"

I shook my head. "No actually the farthest south I've ever been is—"

"Sav." My name said in that tone was all too achingly familiar. I clenched my teeth together, already seeing the next thirty seconds play out in my mind. I took an automatic step back from the nice boy in front of me, knowing that the more distance I put between us the easier it would be to distract Nate. "Can I help you, man?" He walked up and got in between Keaton, my fleetingly new friend, and me.

Keaton looked past the angry shield of a human in front of me, confusion in his eyes. "We were just talking, man." He glanced back to Nate, meeting his gaze and by doing that Keaton made a big mistake. "There's no reason to talk to her like that. She wasn't doing anything wrong. We met the other day at—"

"Nathan. Leave him alone." Jeremy stepped up beside me, his hand reaching out to rest on the top of my ass for a brief wonderful moment, letting me know he was there and I wasn't going to have to go at it alone this time.

My heart was pounding. There were so many things wrong with this moment. Nate was angry for no reason, feeling jealous and possessive. Keaton had almost unintentionally blabbed about seeing me at the lake party I'd lied about. As if the imminent combustion wasn't enough, my body was responding to Jeremy's touch like a damn live wire.

Nate turned around, staring down his older brother. Jeremy wanted to stop a fight from happening. Wanted to stop Keaton from outing us by telling Nate I was at the lake. Jeremy did something no one had ever done before, he cut off Nate, which saved me the embarrassment and the frustration of calling off my best friend. Like yanking the leash of a nearly out of control dog, I'd have to take him home and calm him down. If he lost control, it was on me to fix it and had been for a long time now.

"He was touching her." Nate voice came out in a low growl, his hands fisted at his side. He wanted to hit Keaton, and was itching for a fight. That tone, the tension in his corded muscles. They were telltale signs that Nate's incredibly short fuse was about to ignite.

I could see the confusion in Keaton's face. He'd touched me at the lake. We'd danced and laughed. I'd been free and fun. I'd moved my body against his. Now he was getting in trouble for the small a meaningless gesture of shaking hands. Insanity.

I put my hand on Nate's shoulder, trying to soothe him before things got any more out of hand than they already were. There was a crowd drawing in, moths to the flame of drama. He ignored my silent request, stepping closer to Keaton instead. "You touch her again, and I'll break your fucking neck."

"Nate. Please don't do this." I stepped into his side, whispering against his shoulder. "Let's get out of here." He held his ground, his muscles rigid and his jaw clenched. "Take me home, okay?" I let out the breath I'd been holding when I felt him begin to relax under my hand. I'd said the magic words, I'd chosen him. I'd chosen peace and quiet. I'd rescued him from himself, and saved the people at the party who'd all suffer from his explosion.

As was my lot in life.

Nate stared Keaton down for another few seconds, towering over him, intimidation written in his body language. I tugged on his hand one more time, and he finally turned his back to Keaton, and put his arm around my neck. Nate kept me close as he led me back into the house and away from my small moment of freedom.

I looked over my shoulder and mouthed *I'm sorry* to Keaton, made eye contact with Jeremy, and then hung my head.

I was so dumb to think that tonight would end any other way than it had.

Nate didn't party, and Nate didn't share.

He also never asked me what I wanted, or seemed to care.

It was, and always had been, all about him.

Chapter Fourteen

Jeremy

Savy's life wasn't her own. In retrospect, I'd always kind of assumed that was the case. Recently, I'd seen the way she was with Nathan. How she "managed" him to keep the peace. How she let her wants and needs get more than back-burnered: the damn pilot light never even came on when it came to her happiness. Tonight, I'd seen a smiling, free-spirited girl wilt under the weight of putting my little brother before herself. I'd watched firsthand as he'd stolen the light out of her eyes. He'd been a possessive asshole for no fucking reason at all, and she'd folded for the good of everyone around her. She'd put me, Keaton, and Nathan before herself without even blinking. None of us deserved her, not a single person in her life deserved the devotion she gave so fucking freely. How had her parents, my mom…how had they let this happen? How had they allowed this to be her life? Were they blind, or simply that damn selfish?

"Snap out of it." Max slapped me on the back of the head as he sat down, handing me another cup of beer. I wasn't sure how long I'd been sitting in a lounge chair, staring at the pool and contemplating my next move, but the beer was needed, as was the distraction.

"Thanks, man." Nathan had taken Savy back to her house a while ago, and he hadn't returned to the party. Not that I expected him to.

I wasn't worried about Savy's safety. Nathan would never hurt her. Never in a million fucking years. Well, that wasn't exactly true. While he wouldn't hurt her physically, he'd crushed her emotionally.

She was a prisoner in her own room right now. I could look up from where I was sitting and see into her bedroom window. I didn't, though. I didn't want to see her staring back at me, looking lost and sad. I was chicken-shit and there was nothing I could do to save her right now, no matter how badly I wanted to.

"You shouldn't have gone there with her, and you know it." Max had recognized immediately that things had turned physical when he saw us together earlier tonight. He'd noticed my fingers rubbing her wrist.

I'd steered him outside earlier, when he commented on us holding hands in the middle of the party, and he'd given me a stern five minute lecture.

Apparently our conversation wasn't over yet.

"I thought the plan was *simple*? Show her a good time, let her party a little, and then send her off to Emerson with a tan and little more knowledge about the real world. What the hell happened?"

I sighed, done with pretending, Max wouldn't share our secret with anyone. "I didn't have a lot of choice in the matter—"

"I find that unlikely."

I ignored his sarcastic interruption. "Savy decided she wanted a hook up, she wanted a friend with *all* the benefits. She wanted to know what it felt like to be kissed." I took a deep pull off the beer in my cup. "What else could I do?"

"Tell her no."

I scoffed. "What would've happened if she'd found someone else? What if she got hurt? What if Nathan found out? He'd kill anyone who touched her. You saw him tonight, and that was nothing. The way I've touched her...the way I want to touch her." I shook my head. "He'd lose his mind, man. He'd end up in handcuffs."

Savy could bring him back from the brink, I'd seen her do since we were kids. I wasn't naïve. There was a point when there was no reaching him. A point where he'd snap and no amount of begging from his savior would make a difference.

"So you're sacrificing yourself? Helping Savy, *just* to help her? Putting your life on the line? How selfless of you." He was being an asshole, and I sort of wanted to punch him in his smug face.

"Nathan won't hurt me. I'm his big brother." I looked down in my cup, it was empty again. "I owe this to Savy."

He tilted his head back, laughing loudly. "You owe her this? Are you serious right now? You want this as much as she does, and we both know it. She's gorgeous, pure and forbidden as hell. She's every guys' fucking wet dream."

I clenched my teeth, I didn't like hearing him talk about her like that. "She's more than that. It was either she do this with me, or she finds some random asshole." I stared at Max. "Like you, for example."

He shook his head.

If it wasn't me, it'd be someone else, and as much as I tried to rationalize what I was doing, I knew better. I wanted her fiercely. If someone acted on the same feeling, Nathan would kill them if he ever found out. At least with me, I knew I'd live through it, no matter what. Plus, Savy needed me. She needed me to help her, to show her how to exist without Nathan controlling her every thought and action.

"You want her."

"Everyone wants her." I shot back, suddenly feeling confused and so fucking tried. "That's what you said, right?"

"You can't keep her, Jeremy."

I nodded, getting to my feet for another refill. "I don't intend to."

***

I blamed it on the beer. It had to be the beer, and maybe a little bit of the hormones. I tapped on Savy's window, then waited precariously on the limb of a tree for her to wake up and let me in. I was surprised when Nathan had come home a few hours ago, went straight to his room and didn't come back out. I'd assumed that when he and Savy left the party, he'd be spending the night at her house again. Uninvited as fuck. I leaned forward, the branch bouncing under my weight as I tapped again. Harder. I was horny. I missed her, and I was too buzzed to care that me *missing* her, was a bad sign. I raised my hand, about to tap again—"

"What the hell are you doing?"

I fell forward into Savy's bedroom, the momentum from my almost knock making me crash onto her carpet and take out a stack of books with my head. "Ouch."

I rolled over onto my back, peering up at her. She was wearing a t-shirt and nothing else. Her hair was braided to the side, her face scrubbed clean. I eyed her legs, taking my fill. They were bare, and my fingers inched to trail up to the apex of her perfect thighs.

"What are you doing scaling the side of my house?" Her hands were on her hips as she glared down at my prone form. "You could have been hurt. Or worse. Caught."

I held my hands out to her, and when she went to help me up, I pulled her down next to me instead. "I wanted to make sure you were all right. Make sure everything had gone okay after Nathan brought you home."

We were both laying on our backs, staring at some glow in the dark stars on her ceiling. She sighed and leaned her cheek against my arm. "Well, I was embarrassed, being led out of a party by my best friend like I was a child. Then when we got here, he tried to kiss me."

I propped myself up on my elbow. My eyes had gone wide and my mouth was hanging open. "What?"

She turned on her side to face me, mirroring my position. "Yep."

My heart sank, along with my stomach, and my buzz evaporated. "Did you, um, did you kiss him back?"

The thought of Nathan kissing Savy made me a little crazy and incredibly sad. If he kissed her, and she liked it, if he turned her on I was obsolete. Nathan would give Savy anything she desired, except freedom, of course. But if her *heart* was set on experience and a causal hook-up, he'd do it. No questions asked. On the flip side, if Savy shot him down, his ego would be bruised, *his* heart no doubt hurting. While any scenario where Savannah was with another guy got under my skin and made it crawl, at the end of the day, Nathan was my little brother. I didn't want him to be in pain.

"No." Her voice was quiet and sounded miserable and tortured. "I moved and he got the corner of my mouth. He played it off like that was where he intended to kiss me. But it wasn't. Nate has never gone in like that. He said something over lunch the other day about wanting our relationship to change. I think he wants more."

"Why now?" I glanced from her beautiful eyes to her gorgeous lips. Did he know? Could he tell there was someone else occupying her time and her mind?

She mirrored my gaze, lingering on my mouth as she answered me. "I don't know." She smiled when I reached out and placed my palm on her smooth cheek. "Maybe because we're done with school. Maybe because I'm pushing separate colleges. Maybe he can tell I'm changing. Pulling away. Maybe he can sense I'm happier." She shrugged one shoulder. "Any of those things, all of them perhaps."

"Are you happy?" That was all I wanted for her, to be happy. Sitting in her attic, listening to her talk about her life, it'd been depressing. I'd wanted her to live, to breath easily, to shine. I never wanted to fuck up her life, make it more complicated than it was already. Yet, every day, it seemed like that was what I was doing. "Am I making things harder on you? Making you lie to Nathan, making you sneak around and reject him."

She leaned into my touch, closing her eyes like she was reveling in it. "I'm happier than any time I can remember." She turned and kissed my palm. "Please don't take this away from me. I have seven more weeks, living next door to my best friend. I want to cherish that, but if you leave, if we stop, I'll never make it."

She was happy. She needed me.

That was all I needed to hear.

I dipped down, taking her lips with mine. Doing exactly what I'd had in mind when I scaled the side of her house and fell through her bedroom window. I ran my tongue along the seam of her lips, asking to be let in. She didn't hesitate. She opened for me, matching me in intensity.

She got greedy, and grabbed my hips, pulling me closer. I gave her what she wanted, rolling on top of her. I settled between her legs like it was the hundredth time I was doing it, not the first. She felt so good, so fucking perfect, like she was made only for me. I kissed down the column of her neck, her collarbone, her shoulder. She was panting in my ear, writhing under me.

"Savy, I—"

"Touch me, Jeremy."

We were both out of breath, both desperate for more. I brushed my thumb over her nipple, then took her breast in my hand. She wasn't wearing a bra. I grabbed the hem of her shirt, pulling it off and tossing it behind me. I paused when I felt her body stiffen against mine. "Was that okay? I thought you wanted—"

"I do. I...uh, I... No one's ever seen me like this and, um, I..." She let her words trail off, closing her eyes and then giggling like she was nervous.

I loved moments like these, moments when I got be with her for these firsts. It made everything feel brand new. Like I was getting a second chance at my first time.

"Look at me, Savannah." I kept my voice soft. I wanted her to hear the awe in it. And yeah, I didn't want to wake up her parents. They may be okay with Nathan sleeping in her bed, but I doubted they'd be okay with me getting her naked on her bedroom floor. I waited until her gaze met mine. "You are so fucking perfect. So gorgeous. I don't ever want you to feel uncomfortable or embarrassed with me, okay?" She nodded, biting down on that bottom lip of hers. "If you want to stop, all you have to do is tell me." She nodded again. I smirked. "Do you want to stop?"

She shook her head. "No."

Chapter Fifteen

Savy

I didn't want Jeremy to stop. Ever. I'd never felt so good. I'd never wanted anyone the way I wanted him. I'd never craved a kiss, or a touch. When I was with him, all sense seemed to leave my brain, all reason. I couldn't find it in me to care, not anymore. I deserved these moments, these experiences, and I was done denying myself. If Jeremy was all in, so was I. "Please don't stop."

He dipped his head to my chest, slowly, taking my nipple into the heat of his mouth. My hands automatically threaded through his dark hair. I held him close, making sure he stayed right where he was. My core was clenching with every tug of his skilled lips. It felt explosive. "Your skin tastes like candy." He moved to my other breast and I had to move one palm to my mouth to keep from moaning out loud and risk waking my parents.

We stayed like that, on the floor, fooling around like I was sure all the other kids I went to school with did. It was so...normal. We touched and kissed and teased. He never tried to take it any further than that. One step at a time was exactly what I wanted. Or exactly what I could handle. He seemed to know that. Jeremy was making sure I got what I wanted without pushing. He was everything I needed.

All too soon he pulled back, my mouth felt swollen from his kisses. "I think I should be heading home."

"Well, if you leave now, you'll have to shimmy back down the tree." I bit my lower lip, almost nervous. "You could stay, if you want." I reached over and grabbed my shirt, pulling it over my head to hide the nakedness that was starting to embarrass me all over again. "My parents leave really early for work. They won't check on me now that school's out."

Jeremy stood, reaching down to grab my hands and help me to my feet. "As much as I would love to stay, I think it's best if I go." He peered into my eyes, a smirk on his lips. "One step at a time, wild one." He kissed me again, hooking an arm around my waist and dragging my body against his one more time before crossing the room to open my window. "Same time tomorrow night?"

I narrowed my eyes in disbelief. "You're going to climb back into my window tomorrow night?"

He smirked. "Well, Nathan isn't working tomorrow so I won't be able to see you during the day, and I'll be damned if I go more than twenty-four hours without kissing those sweet lips of yours." He winked. "You wanted a fling? Well, you got it, baby."

I leaned out the window, watching him climb back down the tree, jog across the yard, and disappear into his backyard. I didn't want him to go, but I understood why he didn't stay. I appreciated that he was willing to take things slow when it came to our hook-up.

When Nate had led me out of the party earlier, I'd been embarrassed. But more than that, I'd been scared. Scared that Jeremy would change his mind. That Nate's behavior would remind him how delicate the balance was when it came to his brother.

I knew Jeremy wasn't mine to keep. I knew one day soon this would be over.

I was so damn grateful that day wasn't today.

***

"You want to go to dinner tonight? Maybe down at the Dock?" Nate was lying on the floor in my room, tossing a baseball into the air and then catching it again. He'd brought that ball over here when he was ten, when he'd still been allowed to play team sports. He messed with it all the time. Tossing it in the air, catching it on the back side of his fingers. It was something he did when he was feeling uncomfortable or nervous.

"The Dock? I thought you hated that place."

Nate and I'd had dinner together thousands of times. The only time we went to the Dock was for special occasions with our parents. It was a nice restaurant and we always had to dress up, which was something he didn't like doing. I had the sinking feeling he wanted to eat there because this was a date. My heart started to beat faster at the thought. He was changing his routine, and it was making me nervous. After all our years together, I had come to know exactly what to expect when it came to Nate Deacon. But over the last week or so, he'd been doing and saying things that were throwing me off balance.

"I don't hate it." He tossed the ball again. "I know *you* like it, so, I thought I'd take you." Catch. "About last night." Toss. "I just...that guy, Keaton. I've seen him around school. He's not always a nice guy, Sav."

My mouth was dry, my chest aching like I had a bad case of indigestion. Nate rarely brought up his outbursts after the fact. Usually, he acted like they never happened. He swept them under the rug and moved on as if his bad behavior didn't actually register with him, like he didn't see the harm in most of his interactions with other people. Although, to be fair, I never called him on them either. I guess I was as much at fault as he was. No one held Nate accountable, not even me most days. Still, he was being weird. Or more like, he was being normal, which was weird for him.

"What's going on with you?"

He sat and faced me, looking up from his spot on the floor. "I don't want to lose you."

I tried to smile, despite how uncomfortable I felt. "I've told you over and over, you aren't going to lose me. We're family. I'm not going anywhere." I wiped my sweaty palms on my thighs.

"But you are. You're going to Emerson, and you don't want me to come with you. You want to go to parties, and talk to strangers. Suddenly, you want to do all these things and I feel like either I do them with you, or I'll lose you."

Suddenly? That wasn't true. I'd always wanted to do all the things. I'd been craving the normal high school experience. I wasn't granted that luxury, or rather I hadn't asserted myself to let Nate know I wanted that for myself.

I couldn't pinpoint the moment I'd decided to make my life all about Nathan Deacon. Maybe it was being dragged out of that slumber party in the middle of the night to quiet his nightmares. Maybe it was the guy he'd punched for kissing me. Maybe it was the meltdown he'd had when I told him I wanted to go to a sleep away summer camp. Maybe it was everything, day after day, piled on top of each other. Slowly, without even noticing it—though, to be honest, I felt it, but didn't acknowledge my feelings—I'd been buried under the weight of everything Nate. I hadn't realized it happening until I looked back and I'd let having a life in high school slip right by.

It didn't matter now. The damage was done. I was going to have deal with the fallout.

"It's not that I don't want you to come." I stood up and started pacing my room. "It's not a good enough school for you. You got into *Yale*, which is where you always talked about going. I want what's best for you, and that's not Emerson." I took a deep breath, pausing to face him. "I don't want to get dressed up and go to the Dock. I want to wear shorts and eat a burger. I don't want to go to parties and talk to strangers. I want hang out with you." All partial truths, all semi honest statements. I didn't want to go to the Dock with him. It sounded too much like a date, and that was terrifying, I couldn't date Nathan, not ever. I didn't necessarily want to talk to strangers, though if I did want to chat at a party to someone new, I didn't want World War Three to start if I did.

"Okay, how about a movie at the theater?" He sounded so unsure of himself, so lost. Going out of his comfort zone was difficult for him, but he was making an effort, for me.

I smiled again, and this time it was real. I held my hand out to help him off the floor. "A movie sounds great."

In theory it did. A movie with my best friend, why not? But, as he held onto my hand a little longer than he normally would have, as he pulled me closer to him, instead of letting go, my heart sank. Nate wanted more. There was no denying it. He wanted something I could never give him.

Maybe if things had been different growing up, if I hadn't been charged as his keeper, perhaps I would've fallen in love with him. If the darkest parts of him didn't rest on my shoulders, maybe I wouldn't have felt so weighed down by his affection. As it was, the damage was done.

It wasn't his fault, not really. It was his mom's, or my parents. It was school counselors and family physicians. It was every adult who wouldn't put their foot down and demand that Nate get more help. It was everyone that looked to a child, a little girl, to calm the storm inside her best friend. Salve his irrational anger. Something a child should never have the responsibility of doing.

I couldn't change the past, but I also wouldn't let him control my future.

As fiercely as I loved Nate, I wouldn't allow that love to keep me prisoner anymore.

For once in my life, I was choosing me.

Chapter Sixteen

Jeremy

Long after it'd gotten dark, the night was still heavy with heat. Summer was pressing down on us, making the air feel thick. Partying was the last thing I felt like doing, but sitting at home wallowing and watching the clock was too pathetic to bear. Nathan and Savy went to the movies, she'd texted me their plans that afternoon.

I'm going to hang with Nate tonight.

Do you WANT to hang with him, or is he forcing himself on you?

He's still my best friend. Spending time with him isn't a hardship.

Yeah? If you could choose to do anything, right at this moment, what would it be?

Swimming at the lake. It's hot as hell today. But going to the movies with my best friend is an easily close second.

I'll see you later.

Okay.

That was hours ago, and I'd read and re-read her texts enough that I'd memorized them. I'd gotten so utterly disgusted with myself that I decided to get off my ass and do something to distract myself. Savy was happy to be spending time with Nathan, she'd said so herself twice. I needed to back off and remember my role in her life, and remember my role in Nathan's too. So I did what any typical guy home for summer vacation would do. I hit the nearest party. Booze and random chicks I hadn't seen in over a year, perfect remedy for what was ailing me.

"Hey man, what are you doing here?" Max's threw his arms wide when he noticed me moving between cars, making my way to where he was posted up. "I figured you'd be off making a bigger mess of things with Savannah."

I shoved Max's hand out of the way instead of giving him the five he was requesting. "Fuck off."

"Mighty testy tonight, aren't we?" He grabbed a beer out of the cooler in the bed of his truck behind him and tossed it to me. "Not having her by your side is affecting your mood now?" He tsked, shaking his head like he was disappointed. "Shameful, bro."

I popped the top and drained half of the cold brew in a few swallows. I hated that Max was right, and I hated even more that Savy wasn't here. It wasn't that she was at the movies with Nathan, it was that she wasn't with *me*. That right there was a big fucking problem. I'd never admit it out loud. I wouldn't give Max the satisfaction.

"Not *testy* at all. Who the hell uses the word testy? What are you? Eighty?"

"She with Nathan?" Max studied a group of girls grinding on each other down by the lake shore. They were putting on a hell of a show, hopping to be noticed.

I followed his gaze, watching for a few seconds, hoping one of them would seem like a good idea. But *none* of them stirred anything inside me. They didn't hold a candle to Savy, and I was exactly as shameful as Max accused me of being. "Yeah, they're at the movies."

Max grinned, his smile tight and sarcastic as fuck. "Well, he *is* her best friend."

I hung my head. There was no denying that. "That he is." He was her best friend and my baby brother. I was the asshole sitting here wishing like hell that they weren't enjoying their time together.

Max added, "*And* your little brother." Like he was reading my mind or some shit. Sometimes it sucked having lifelong friends who knew you better than you knew yourself.

"Please, man. I really don't want another lecture tonight." I tossed back the rest of my beer, crushing it in my hand and then helping myself to another. I hadn't talked to Savy for hours. By now, the movie should be over, and Nathan should've brought her home. I wanted to be climbing in her window about now, but I wasn't. That pissed me off.

"All I'm saying is that jealousy doesn't look good on you." Max hopped down off his tailgate, eyeing the girls still dancing on the shoreline.

"I'm not jealous." I looked past him, eyeing the attention seeking group again, silently praying for one of them to make me *want* the way Savy did. "I'm horny." Lies, both of those statements. Well, not both. I was horny. Unfortunately, the only girl that could cure my ache was on a date with my little brother.

"Sure you are man." He glanced at me then back to the girls. "Seems if you really wanted to cure those blue balls, those chicks would be able to help you out a lot better than Savannah would, yeah?"

I scoffed, trying to buy myself an alibi. "How old are those chicks? They don't even look legal."

He grinned, like the cat that was about to eat the canary. "Old enough to know better, I guarantee you."

***

I still didn't know if Nathan was at home or at Savy's. That was the only reason I wasn't currently scaling the tree on the side of her house. It was well past midnight and my little brother wasn't answering his phone. I'd texted, and I'd called. Nothing. I'd fought the urge to contact Savy the whole Uber ride home. But I was afraid that he'd still be with her and he'd see my name pop up on her phone. I wasn't scared of my brother, I simply didn't want to ruin Nathan and Savy's friendship. At least that's what I kept telling myself as I walked into my dark house.

I went straight to Nathan's room, letting out a relieved breath when I found him lying on his bed. He was still dressed, stretched out over his covers, he'd obviously gotten home not too long ago.

When he saw me he used the remote control in his hand to turn down the documentary he was watching. "Hey."

I leaned against his doorframe, already sneaking out of my room and into Savy's in my mind. "How was your day off?"

He smirked, which was typical, I never really got a full smile out of him. "Spent it with Sav, so it was fucking fantastic."

I wanted to punch him in his stupid smirking face. "What did you guys do?" But instead, I tried like hell to play it cool.

He raised an eyebrow in disbelief. I'd never cared to ask before, and he knew it. "We hung out, went to dinner then a movie."

I glanced down at my phone, checking the time. "You just now getting home?"

"Yeah. Why? You my keeper now?"

I wanted to scream at him. I wanted to go off and tell him that job had always fallen to the girl next door. The child that our family had used as a human buffer. An instrument, a shield. But I couldn't do that since I was the asshole stealing time with the girl my brother needed to stay sane.

I swallowed my anger, making sure my voice was even and unaffected. "No. Curious, that's all." I pushed away from his room, calling, "Goodnight," over my shoulder. I closed my bedroom door and threw the lock. I opened my window slowly, trying like hell to make sure it didn't make any noise before I jumped the few feet to the soft green grass below.

My heart was pounding. I was so damn excited to see her, to hold her, to kiss her. I couldn't stop smiling. I sprinted across our yards, swinging up into the tree I'd used last night. She'd left her window open halfway for me, which meant this time I wasn't going to fall into a tuck and roll.

Savy was lying in her bed, asleep with soft lamplight across her pretty face. Her long dark lashes rested against her cheeks, she looked like fucking Sleeping Beauty. I went to her door, turning the lock in place to make sure her parents wouldn't surprise us. Then I crossed the room, standing over her for a moment, drinking her in. When I couldn't stand it any longer, I dipped down and placed a soft kiss to her lips.

She smiled, her eyes slowly fluttering open. "Hey. I didn't know if you'd come." She scooted over, making room for me beside her in bed.

I knew it was probably dangerous, I knew I'd have a hard time controlling myself, but I couldn't turn her down. I wanted to lie next to her, I wanted to become part of her space and be surrounded by her scent. I wanted to erase every trace of my brother from her skin, from her room. As much as I tried to deny it, to fight it, I'd accidentally made Savy mine.

There was no going back now.

I stepped out of my shoes and pulled my shirt off, tossing it to the floor before climbing into bed next to the most beautiful girl in the world. "I'm sorry it took me so long." I kissed the top of her head when she snuggled into my chest. "Nathan wouldn't answer his phone and I didn't know if he was still here."

She gazed up at me, her eyes sad, swimming with unshed tears and breaking my heart. "I think Nate wants to date me. He keeps trying to take me out to nice restaurants and hold my hand. There's been more than once when I was afraid he was going to try to kiss me again."

I'd always known that Nathan had feelings for Savy, it was clear as day. When I decided to be Savy's "hook-up" I figured if they weren't dating by now, neither of them thought it was a good idea. A justification, for sure, the truth was, Nathan was in love with Savy, and the thought of losing her was making him hold on tighter than ever. I couldn't blame him. Wasn't that what I was doing as well?

I swallowed past the lump in my throat. "Do you want to date him? Do you want Nathan?"

I was terrified of her answer. Somehow over the last week, somehow between the attic to lying in her bed tonight, I'd messed up. I'd started to fall for her. I thought of her as mine, and I didn't want to share anymore. Not with my brother or anyone else. But if Nathan was who Savy wanted, then I'd walk away and try to be happy for them.

She pushed up on her elbow and leaned over me. "No. I don't want to date Nate. I don't want to kiss him or sleep next to him all night. It's not Nate, it never has been." Her gaze moved from mine down to my lips. "It never will be."

I held my breath waiting for her to take charge, waiting for her to make the first move this time.

Thank god, she did.

Chapter Seventeen

Savy

My heart was pounding as I dipped down and touched my lips to his. This was me taking what I wanted, initiating instead of waiting for something to happen to me. I wasn't reacting, I was causing what would happen next. The thrill of being in charge, of having dominion over the guy I'd wanted since I was a kid, was an intoxicating kind of power. I put my hand on his cheek, kissing him deeply. I took a chance, biting his lower lip playfully and suddenly I was on my back with him towering over me.

His eyes were dark, his breathing ragged. "You're so fucking beautiful, Savy."

His words were soft, whispered across my lips, making my heart flutter in my chest. I never knew that this was what I'd been missing. I never knew how light a person could feel, how free while being tethered by wonderful emotions. The kind that made my blood bubble, not my stomach churn. Jeremy was showing me the whole world, and I wanted to chase this desire inside me to the ends of the earth.

I wrapped my arms around his neck, pulling him down so I could kiss him again. His weight rested on top of me, his hips settled between mine. I could feel him, rigid against my core. I arched my back, grinding against him, testing out how it felt to seek my own pleasure. He groaned into my mouth, his tongue tangling with mine.

I moved my hands down his sides, reveling in the feel of his warm flesh over hard muscle. I wanted to feel his skin on mine, his heat, I wanted to feel all of him. His eyes searched mine, silently asking for permission and waiting until I nodded before dragging my nightgown off my overheated body.

"You call the shots, okay? You tell me when you've had enough." Jeremy brushed my hair off my face, smiling as he spoke softly in the dark. "You say the word and I'll kiss you good night and go home, no pressure."

I shook my head. "I don't want you to go home." I let my hand slide between our bodies, palming his length, surprised at my boldness. "I want you to stay with me all night." I wasn't sure how to voice what I wanted. I was almost afraid he'd tell me no, that he'd tell me I wasn't ready. He'd already told me once that he wasn't going to have sex with me, but things were different now, we were different. I wanted all of him and I was pretty sure he felt the same way.

He closed his eyes, biting his bottom lip in a way that drove me crazy. "I need you to be clear about what you're telling me, Savy."

I took a deep breath, my sensitive nipples rubbing against his chest. "I want you to be my first."

"Savy." His eyes closed, his lungs expanding and pressing down on me. "That's skipping a couple steps, baby."

That wasn't a no. He didn't immediately refuse, which meant he was no longer opposed to the idea. His answer gave me hope, made me confident enough to push for more. "We have a few weeks left, right? We could always back track."

"There's no need to rush, we—"

"I'm not rushing." I took his face in my hands and he opened his eyes. "I know what I want, and I want you. Right now. In this all-consuming, can't think straight, messy way. I want to be young and in lust. I don't want to wait."

Jeremy took a deep breath, chill bumps breaking out across his flesh. I watched, waiting to see if he would give me what I wanted, what we both wanted. "I don't deserve this from you." His tone was soft, and his words were sweet.

"It's yours. It's always belonged to you." My first crush, my first everything. It felt right. It felt perfect.

Slowly, he lifted his body off mine, shucked off his jeans, then reached inside his back pocket and pulled out his wallet. A moment later, he was kneeling between my legs, rolling a condom over his hard cock.

He crawled back up my body, and started kissing his way to my lips, nibbling up my neck, and nipping at my earlobe before brushing his mouth across my cheek. My eyes were wide open, watching every move he made, not wanting to miss a thing. My fingers traced his face as he settled back between my thighs. The fear and excitement pulsing through my body made me shiver. He paused, pulling my covers up over his shoulders, cocooning us both. "You sure?"

I nodded. My lip caught between my teeth.

He bent down and nipped my collarbone before using his expert tongue on my nipples. I began writhing, the feeling was so exquisite. As he sucked a nipple into his mouth, he positioned himself at my entrance and began pushing inside me slowly.

Everything about what we were doing was so foreign and for a brief moment my nerves got the better of me. He stopped, raised his head and began kissing me, spearing his tongue inside my mouth. When he felt me relax, he continued his gentle invasion, and slowly the sting faded and I shuddered, a moan escaping my lips as he started to carefully move inside me. The fullness wasn't so odd anymore, it was welcome.

I gripped his hips, my back arching without me thinking to do it. I wanted him inside me forever, I never wanted this to stop. I couldn't go back to being so empty when being consumed by Jeremy made me feel so alive.

"You okay?" he whispered against my ear, his hips thrusting slowly, his arms tense as he held himself above me.

I nodded again. "Yes." My words came out with a whimper. "I'm good. I'm really good." I shifted beneath him, testing my rhythm with small movements until I was meeting his measured thrusts with my own. "I'm good. I promise, please…uh, god, please don't stop."

He kissed me again, pushing into me harder while catching my moans with his mouth. "Fuck, baby, you've got to be quieter." He put his finger to my lips, a smirk on his face.

I didn't care that my parents were downstairs. Nothing in this world mattered more than what was happening between me and Jeremy in this moment. My body felt like a livewire, electricity shooting through every nerve ending I possessed. "Savy, fuck, you feel so good."

I moaned again, hiking my thighs higher on his hips. I could feel the heat building, my release about to consume me. I dug my nails into his arms, wanting more and not knowing how to form the words. He pulled back and slammed into me, making me cry out in pleasure. "Yeah. Oh, god. Please...don't, oh, oh." I was babbling incoherent fragments, but somehow he understood me.

He chuckled, his sexy smirk still in place as he gently put his hand over my mouth before he slammed back into me again. I nodded, and he kept going, letting go of all the control he was harnessing to keep from hurting me.

He moved inside me over and over, relentless until I cried his name against the palm of his hand. His whole body tensed as my orgasm stole all my senses.

***

The sun was coming up, the dark purple sky slowing becoming pink. I'd spent the whole night wrapped in Jeremy's arms. He'd been perfect, kind, and careful. Then he'd held me so tight. I knew that he needed to wake up, that he needed to get home before anyone noticed that he was missing. My parents would freak if they found us naked under my sheets. Although, they never batted an eye when Nate stayed over. I silently wondered if they'd be mad simply because it was Jeremy, or if they'd be mad because of the possible fallout that would ensue if Nate ever found out.

Would they be worried for me, or would they be worried for themselves and for their friend, Jeremy and Nate's mom? Not knowing the answer to my own questions pissed me off, but it didn't change the fact that all hell would break loose if Jeremy didn't get home soon.

I turned to look at him, running my fingers through his hair. He was gorgeous. His dark looks weren't broody, but sexy. He was about having fun, being easy-going, gobbling up life and enjoying the ride. He was everything his brother wasn't. I closed my eyes, shoving thoughts of Nate to the farthest corners of my mind. I couldn't think of him now, I wasn't ready for the guilt to come creeping in trying to steal my joy. "Hey, Jeremy? It's morning. It's time for you to go."

He groaned, pulling my body closer to him. "I don't wanna go."

"I don't want you to go either." I rolled to my side, biting my lips together when I felt him hard against my thigh. I knew I had to be blushing, which was so stupid after everything that happened last night. "Nate will be up soon, we're supposed to run together."

It was the heat of summer, if we didn't run with the sunrise, we wouldn't be able to run at all. I sat up, holding my sheet to my chest. My comforter had somehow ended up on the floor, the thin sheet the only thing covering our still naked bodies. I looked down, my cheeks heating when I noticed the blood staining them. I started making a list of the things I needed to do in my head. Bleach my sheets was number one. Get on birth control would probably be a good number two, because I wanted a repeat of last night…several of them.

"What's going on in that pretty head of yours?" Jeremy sat up next to me, kissing my bare shoulder and sending chills racing down my exposed spine.

I quickly grabbed the thicker blanket from the floor, trying to cover my bloody sheets. I didn't know why I found it so embarrassing, but I did. "I, uh, I need to get cleaned up before—"

"Hey." Jeremy rested his palm softly on my cheek, making me look into his eyes. "Tell me how you're feeling, please baby."

My breath shuttered at the adoration in his chocolate brown eyes. Jeremy was a good man, and I suddenly felt incredibly lucky that he was the guy I'd waited for. "I'm feeling bummed out that you have to go, I'm feeling nervous that Nate is going to take one look at me and know what I did last night. I'm feeling embarrassed that there is blood on my sheets, and I'm feeling thankful that it's you who is here with me. I can't imagine it being anyone else."

His bright smile warmed me to my core. "Leaving right now is the last thing I want to do." He kissed my shoulder again, then moved to the column of my neck, and the corner of my mouth before pulling back. "I'd love nothing more than to stay in this bed with you for another few hours, wait for your parents to leave so I could hear you whisper my name as I make you come over and over again." If I thought I was blushing before, it was nothing compared to the heat and desire Jeremy's words had stirred in me. "As for your sheets, there's nothing to be embarrassed about, baby." He shook his head, his expression playful. "So you know, I'm feeling pretty fucking thankful that it was me too."

I rested my forehead against his, grinning as he trailed his fingertips down my back. "You should go."

I felt him nod. "On one condition."

"What's that?" I pulled away, wondering if the smile on my face would ever dim.

"Leave your window open again tonight?"

I nodded as I watched Jeremy climb out of my bed and search the floor for his clothes.

Chapter Eighteen

Jeremy

I climbed into my room through the window, careful not to make a sound and quickly crossed the hall to jump into the shower. I didn't want to wash Savy off my body, there was something about her that made me feel a little primal. Possessive. I'd been with other girls, there was no denying that. But the moment I'd slid inside Savy last night, every other female on the planet ceased to exist. There was only her. She consumed me. Being her first, holding her while she slept. Waking up to her fingers in my hair. I loved every single second of it. All of it. I wanted to do it over and over again. I wanted to be next to her until the moment time ripped us apart.

She wasn't a fling. She wasn't a project. Not anymore. Not after last night.

"Yo, I'm running with Sav, she said it'd be rude not to invite you." Nathan banged on the bathroom door, startling me, which caused soap to run into my eyes. "You in?"

His tone told me he wanted me to be *out*, he wanted to run with Savy alone. He didn't like to share her, and although I assured Savy that Nathan wouldn't know, I was starting to wonder if maybe he would. I should stay home. I should give them time together without the pressure of having me there. I knew that, but I couldn't stay away. I couldn't pass up the chance to see her again. It'd been less than fifteen minutes since I left her bed, and it felt like fifteen hours.

"Yeah, give me five and I'll meet you guys out front."

I shut off the shower, dried off and dressed in record time. I felt light, giddy. The only person who had ever evoked these feelings was the beautiful blonde girl next door. I sighed, hanging my head as

I stepped out the front door to see Nathan grinning at her as they stretched. Yeah, she made my brother feel all those things too, and it was written plain as day across his otherwise perpetually grimacing face.

I was an asshole.

Savy looked up, catching my eye, her bottom lip caught between her perfect teeth. My cock immediately stirred at the sight of her. *Down dude. Now is not the time and she's probably sore anyway.* I joined them, stretching out my hamstrings, letting the music coming from the phone strapped to Savy's arm fill the silence as we took off down the driveway and then to the left, taking the same route we'd taken the last few times we'd all run together.

"Sav, you okay?" Nathan lengthened his stride, easily falling into step beside her. "You're moving a little slow this morning."

Savy's cheeks turned red and I had to chomp down on my cheeks to keep from smirking. It's not that I liked that she was sore, that she was hurting a little, but the reminder of what we'd shared last night had me feeling...a lot of things. Smug, male, horny, guilty, proud. Possessive. All the emotions I never experienced after being with a girl. Savy was different in every possible way.

"I'm fine, I uh, was doing yoga last night after you left and I uh, pulled something." Savy licked her lips, glancing at me before turning her gaze back the pavement on the horizon.

"Why were you doing yoga at midnight?" Nathan still looked concerned, maybe a little confused. All I could think about was the way Savy had felt in my arms, her soft panting breaths in my ear. *Fuck.* My running shorts were not going to hide my dick's reaction to the memories of last night if I didn't calm down.

"I couldn't sleep. Yoga's supposed to be relaxing." She picked up the pace, trying to put some distance between Nathan and her. "Like I said, I'm fine."

I wanted to tell him to leave her alone. I wanted to tell her to take it easy, that she didn't have anything to prove to anyone. But I kept my mouth shut because doing either of those things would only result in more issues. Nathan wouldn't take my advice when it came to his best friend, he had no reason to. My defending her to him would make him see red. Really, he was concerned and was only trying to make sure she was okay.

He loved her. I knew that.

We finished our run without saying another word. The only sound between the three of us was the soft music playing from Savy's phone and the pounding of our shoes on the pavement. My thoughts were on last night, the hours I'd spent with Savy playing on a loop inside my brain. Once we rounded the final corner, bringing us back to our houses, Savy broke off from my brother and me.

"I'm going to grab a shower." She tossed up a little wave and didn't wait for either of us to answer before pushing open her front door and disappearing from sight.

Nathan stopped at the mailbox, grabbing the mail neither of us had bothered to collect while our mom had been out of town. He flipped through the stack, plucking out a thick brochure with Emerson in big purple letters. My jaw clenched, my muscles tensed, and not from the short three miles we'd ran.

"Still thinking about following Savy to a school that has nothing for you?" I could hear the irritation in my voice, and prayed to god that my brother couldn't.

He glanced up from the pages he was flipping through. "Why? You don't want me that close?"

"Why would I care how close you live to Savy next year? It's not like we're going to hang out or anything." I tried to sound bored and unaffected, but the truth was I did care. I cared because Savy needed fucking space. It was bad enough Yale was only two hours from Emerson. I was surprised she hadn't decided to go to UCLA or somewhere else out west.

Nathan's eyes narrowed. "I meant that close to *you.*"

Shit. Of course he did. Because why the hell would Savy even be in my mind at all? My possessive streak was going to get us all in trouble. Northeastern was basically next door to Emerson. "Either way you'll be close to me." I smiled, stepping past him and onto the porch. "You're my brother. We'll see each other no matter what."

He followed me, surprising the crap out of me as he kept talking. "Sav keeps pushing for me to go to Yale." Nathan never let me into his life and certainly not into anything having to do with him and Savy.

I headed into the kitchen, grabbing a bottle of water and then tossing one to him. "She wants what's best for you, and we all know that's Yale." I took a sip of the cool liquid, letting it wash away the irritation lodged in my throat. "You've always wanted to go to Yale.

Dad went to Yale. Savy knows that and I'm sure she doesn't want to be the reason for you to give up that dream." I shrugged. "Maybe she's afraid you'll end up resenting her for it."

"I could never resent, Sav." His eyes were dark, his expression guarded.

I shrugged again, moving past him to hide in my room. "Never is a long time."

I couldn't be a good brother in this situation. I knew that him going to Emerson would be bad for Savy, and I wanted to think that me pushing him toward Yale was simply for her sanity.

But it wasn't, not anymore.

I closed my bedroom door and plucked my cell off the charger, feeling like a shit older brother, and a jealous gossipy "casual hookup." I didn't like either, but I couldn't seem to help it.

Nathan was just thumbing through an Emerson catalogue.

I'd done what I could, like I promised Savy I would. I couldn't make Nathan's decision for him and no one could strong arm him into anything. But maybe, just maybe, I'd given him something to think about.

Great. Well. At least dorms there aren't coed, so we won't be living together.

Living together? Hell to the fucking no. How was I supposed to still see Savy next year if she was…oh. Wow. Well, that was new. When had I decided that I wanted to keep seeing Savy once we headed to Boston? Probably around the same fucking time I'd held her in my arms all night long and used the thump of her heartbeat as the metronome to which I fell asleep.

I did what I could to try to push him toward Yale.

Am I a terrible friend for not wanting to go to the same college?

I glanced at the clock. It'd been fifteen minutes since Savy had broken away from us and went home. That was how long it took for her guilt to set in. How exhausting it must be living with that ever present weight on her shoulders.

You are the farthest thing from a terrible friend. You have taken care of Nathan for most of your life. You don't want him to go to the same college as you for good reasons. It's not like you want him to make a bad choice. You want him to go to Yale, the place where success is in the damn water.

I think he's afraid to be without me. Afraid of what he'll do if I'm not there to keep him even.

She probably wasn't wrong. But the thing was, Nathan wasn't her problem. If Nathan was worried about his impulse control, then he needed to get a therapist in New Haven. He needed to discuss medications that he could benefit from. If Nathan was worried about himself, then that meant he knew he had issues. It was long past time he took some responsibility for his own mental health.

You don't have to be Nathan's keeper. You can't watch out for him the rest of your life. What would that even look like? You think your future husband is going to build on an extra room so Nathan has a place to live?

Don't be silly. Nate would never let me get married.

Well that was the fucking saddest statement I'd heard in a long-ass time. I knew she was sort of kidding, but I also knew there was some fear and truth in her words. If Nathan never backed off, never let her out of his sight, how the hell was she supposed to have a life? Not that I wanted to think of her with other guys. But still. How was she supposed to find a guy to settle down with? Have kids? Join the damn PTA? How was she supposed to live at all with Nathan attached to her side?

Let's do something really dumb tonight.

That sounds ominous.

I was spiraling a bit. Panicked at what her future looked like with Nathan as her shadow. She couldn't and shouldn't have to survive that existence. These had to be the thoughts that plagued her. The thoughts she'd kept to herself the last twelve years. I was sure she had constant anxiety lodged in her chest. Fuck me. This was all so much more of a disaster than I'd ever realized.

Meet me in the driveway at midnight.

You want to me sneak out?

I want you to live, baby.

Chapter Nineteen

Savy

I used the tree to sneak out of my house, climbing down like Jeremy did. I'd never done that before. I'd never left my house while my parents were asleep. I'd never been the rebellious teenager. Nate wouldn't let me be. Saying that now, I know I allowed myself to succumb under the pressure of his expectations. The more I thought about it, the more I was sure I'd taken the easier road with Nate. Pushing back meant the potential of a whole host of reactions, none of them good. Maybe, if I'd started to push back early on, he would've found a way to adjust. Ugh. Water under the bridge. I rolled my eyes, annoyed with the way I'd spent my four years of high school.

I loved Nate, and I had good memories, but I'd never had as much fun as I'd had the last couple of weeks with Jeremy. One brother kept me in a safe padded box, the other was willing to jump off a cliff holding my hand. They were as different as two people could be, and I was lucky to love them both, but in different ways.

"Hey wild one, you ready?" I jumped about a foot in the air, whirling around when Jeremy snuck up behind me. "Whoa, calm down, it's only me."

He wrapped his arms around my waist, pulling me to him and kissing my lips. "You scared me." I giggled, resting my forehead against his chest. "I've never snuck out before."

He hummed, his mouth against my ear. "I love capturing all your firsts, baby."

His words had me blushing in the dark, remembering the way he'd felt moving inside me last night. I wanted him, fiercely, instantly. A few whispered words and I was wanton. "Where are we going?"

He clasped my hand, leading me to his car. He helped me into the passenger seat, settling a heavy backpack on my lap before racing around to the driver's side. "It's a surprise."

We drove through town, the windows down and the radio loud. Well-lit streets gave way to country roads and fields of nothingness on either side. He directed the car off the main road, winding his way through a narrow tree-lined dirt path. We came to a stop in a clearing, and he switched off the lights before killing the engine. The only sound was crickets, the only light coming from our town so far below.

"I've never been here before." Never seemed like all I was capable of thinking and saying. Back to wasted years of living in a bubble.

He chuckled, climbing out of the car and ducking his head back in to grab the bag off my lap. "Well I should think not. This is where horny teenagers come to hook up."

I knew I was blushing with excitement. He helped me out of the car, leading to the edge of the clearing and laying a blanket in the sparse grass. We sat, facing the twinkling lights, drinking from the bottle of red wine he'd opened.

I knocked my shoulder against his after several minutes of shared silence. "Well?"

"Well what?" His hand stroked up and down my back, his movement pausing to play with my hair every now and then.

"We going to be horny teenagers or what?" I giggled when he instantly tackled me to the blanket, attacking my mouth and groping my breasts, he groaned and started to hump my leg.

"Horny enough for you?"

I was still laughing, gasping to catch my breath when he started to tickle me. "Was this what you were like in high school?" I wiggled, trying to get out from under him. "I'm glad I got the college version." He tickled me more, placing sloppy kisses all over my neck and chest.

He pulled back, a happy smile on his incredibly handsome face. "All versions of me are amazing, baby, you know that."

"I do." I wrapped my legs around his waist, peering up at him in the dark.

"Even the most amazing version of me doesn't hold a candle to *any* version of you Savannah Nightingale." He dipped down to kiss me senseless.

We made out under the stars until kisses weren't enough. Then Jeremy slid down my body, pulling off my panties with his teeth before using his mouth and fingers that had me crying out his name into the dark night sky.

Chapter Twenty

Jeremy

We were spread out on my blanket, the wine long forgotten and spilled into the dirt beside us. Savy's head was resting on my chest, my fingers trailing through her beautiful long hair. We'd been quiet for a few minutes, catching our breath while listening to the night sounds around us. I enjoyed every moment I was with Savy, it didn't matter what we were doing. I missed her when we were apart, and I worried about her when she was with my brother. She had slowly consumed me, there was no other word for it.

Maybe I was as possessed as Nathan. Maybe she amplified his crazy, his love for her sending him over the edge of sanity.

"I had a crush on you when we were younger." Savy's sweet voice broke through the silence.

I couldn't help but smile, tugging her hair playfully. "I was pretty wrapped up in my own shit." I know I was selfish. I'd been more than content to let her take on the sole responsibility of Nathan. It wasn't fair of me, but I'd been a kid myself. "I noticed you, Savy, I did. But, not the same way you noticed me, as arrogant as that sounds. You were Nathan's best friend and I didn't want to set him off, you know? I didn't want to upset the balance, I was too afraid what that would mean for *me*." I felt shitty about it. Hell, that was why I'd started hanging out with her in the first place. As a means to right a wrong, as a way to ease my guilty conscience.

Not anymore though. Now I basically worshipped the ground she fucking walked on.

"Are you still worried about setting him off?"

The honest answer was, yes. I was concerned about what would happen if Nathan found out how I felt about his best friend. But lately, I was more concerned what would happen if he *never* found out. How long could Savy and I sneak around like this? She was leaving for school in a few weeks, so was I, and so was Nathan. He hadn't told us yet which school he chose, and he could very well end up on the same campus as Savy. How would that even work?

"I have some reservations about that brother of mine." I leaned forward, unable to keep my lips to myself any longer as I kissed her shoulder. "I'm not ready to give you up, so I push them way into the back of my mind where all the icky stuff lives."

Her blonde eyebrows rose, a smile playing on her pillow soft lips. Lips still puffy from my kisses. "The icky stuff?"

"You know, the scenes from scary movies that stick with you, the one time you walked in on your parents getting it on. That sort of stuff." I chuckled as she wrinkled her nose. "What's in your icky file?"

She sighed, rolling onto her back and exposing her perfect skin to the moon, completely comfortable to be wearing my open shirt. "Nate putting that neighbor kid in a choke hold. Nate crying all night after your dad passed. Nate punching guys who talked to me, Nate dragging me out of that party the other ni—"

"I get it, baby. Nathan is your icky file." I put my palm on her hip, my thumb caressing her skin. I hated that was the way she felt. I hated it for her and for my brother. It was sad, no matter which way you looked at it.

"He's in my good files too, though." She turned her head, her eyes searching mine. "Watching movies, playing in the park, swimming, camp outs, s'mores, popsicles on hot summer days. Until this summer with you, Nate was all my good memories *and* all my icky ones. That's what happens when you have one friend. They become your everything good and bad. I don't remember a time in my life when he wasn't in it, when he wasn't part of every day."

I didn't need to ask Savy the question that came to my mind, the question of whether she'd go back in time to change things if she could. I already knew the answer. She would suffer all over again to help my brother because she loved him, and she had a kind heart. She was selfless when everyone around her was the complete opposite. Or maybe not. Now that she'd had a taste of freedom, maybe she would've tried to expand her horizons while keeping Nathan in check. Stupid to even think about. No one got a do-over.

I studied the night sky, sad to see that the deep purple was developing edges of pink. "We need to get you home, the sun will be up soon."

"When I was younger, I used to dream about you coming through my window and rescuing me." Savy held my gaze. "You'd tell me to pack a bag, that we were going on an adventure." She turned her attention back to the sleeping city below us. "I would wake up torn. In love with the fantasy and guilt ridden for wanting to leave Nate."

"I used to have dreams of you too, but they got a little racier than that." I reached out, trailing my fingertips through her silky hair.

"You're a dream come true, Jeremy."

Her words were like a zap to my soul, filling me with light. I sat up, pulling her back against my chest. "No Savy, you're the dream." I kissed her neck, breathing in her sweet scent. "I promise, baby, one day, I'll get you out of here and we'll go on all the adventures your heart can handle."

As she relaxed in my arms, I went over the words I'd spoken to her. Had I promised Savy a future? Had I promised her forever? This summer with her started with so many boundaries, so many guidelines and expirations. But my feelings for her had grown, like they had a life and a mind of their own. I couldn't find it in me to resist anymore.

"I'm falling in love with you," I said the words softly and against her skin, not afraid to let them out, but wary of the wreckage they could cause.

She leaned in, her hands searching for mine in the growing light. "I think I've been in love with you my whole life."

Chapter Twenty-One

Savy

Jeremy got me home minutes before sunrise, kissing me quickly and sending me back up the tree and through my bedroom window. I collapsed on my mattress, tired but too excited to sleep. Instead I daydreamed, the TV on in the background. I lay there for hours, simply happy to be alone with my thoughts, replaying the last few nights on a constant loop.

Jeremy was falling in love with me, and he'd dreamed about me like I'd dreamed about him. The boy I'd crushed on my whole life loved me back. I couldn't stop smiling, my cheeks hurt from the effort. This summer with Jeremy was more than anything I ever saw coming. One favor for his brother, one night of helping me with a chore my dad wouldn't let go, had turned into an actual dream come true. I felt lucky and giddy. I knew soon the guilt would rise up, like it always did, but for now, I wanted to be eighteen and in love, grinning so big my face ached.

"Savy, sweetheart, Jeremy is here, I'm sending him up." My mom called her warning from the bottom of the stairs, which made me roll my eyes. Neither she nor my father ever gave me a heads up before seeing Nate bound up the stairs and into my room.

I clicked off the TV, surprised he was here in the middle of the day, especially after seeing each hours ago. Nate wasn't working and we had plans soon. I hated that my mind immediately went to Nate, wondering what he was doing and if he'd catch me with his brother. What Jeremy and I did wasn't wrong. Lying by omission was.

"Hey wild one, it's a gorgeous day, why are you locked in your house?" Jeremy dipped down, kissing my lips and leaving me instantly wanting more.

"Someone kept me up all night. I'm exhausted." I scooted over, making room for him to sit next to me. He reached out, stroking my hair and tugging playfully on the ends. "Also, I have plans with Nate in a bit."

Jeremy wrinkled his nose. "Cancel them."

My eyebrows rose in surprise. Jeremy had never demanded I skip out on his brother before. Honestly, I couldn't remember one time in my life when I'd done that. "What? I can't do that." I wanted to. I wanted nothing more than to send a text telling Nate that something came up and we'd have to hang out tomorrow instead. As depressing as the truth was, that wasn't my life. I'd never ditch him. "He's working tonight. We can see each other then."

"Sleepover?" He rolled over, pinning me to my mattress, settling between my thighs and driving me crazy with his sinful kisses and roaming hands. "Say yes. Tell me I can spend all night exploring this perfect body of yours."

"A thousand times, yes." I wrapped my arms around his neck, pulling his lips to mine for more.

We stayed like that, making out in my bed, tempting fate and risking my parents catching us at any moment. I couldn't find it in me to care though. I wanted Jeremy. I wanted his weight on top of me, keeping me grounded in the reality I had options. I wanted his attention and his playfulness.

"Baby, your phone is ringing." Jeremy reached under my butt where my phone had slipped out. Sighing, and sitting up, I said, "It's Nate."

He clicked accept, putting the call on speaker phone and resting it on my chest. He always did that when Nate called, put the call on blast so he could hear the whole conversation. I knew it spoke to his jealousy, and after his admission last night, I felt bad for him. I wished he didn't have to hide us, and that he didn't have to share me.

"Hey Nate, what's up?"

"I got someone to cover my evening shift." He paused, the sound of weights being returned to their resting spots filling the background. "Let's do a movie tonight, we can fall asleep to the TV."

My heart sank. I didn't want Nate in my bed. I didn't want to cancel my plans with Jeremy. Shit, this had been my life for as long as I could remember. I didn't think it was time to change that now. Not when I was so close to gaining my freedom.

"Okay, sure. See you soon?" What I was really asking him was how much time did I have to bask in his brother's arms before he would be here to command the rest of my day.

"I'll be home in a about an hour."

"Okay, drive safe." I pressed end on the call, tossing my phone to the side. I could feel the tension radiating from Jeremy, and I couldn't blame him. This was the first time that Nate had come between us this way. The first time I'd had to literally choose his brother over him. It felt wrong.

"What the fuck?" I winced at his tone. "You complain about him crowding your bed and then you agree that easy?"

"Easy?" I sat up, shaking my head, tears instantly stinging the back of my eyes. "You're crazy if you think any of this is easy, or that I want you to leave. After telling you I want you to spend the night, how could you say that?" It was the last thing I wanted to happen, and he had to know that. He was frustrated and disappointed, and I was right there with him. "Trying to ignore the way Nate touches me is the last way I wanted to spend my—"

"What do you mean the way he touches you?" Jeremy's eyes were hard, his fists clenched. I'd never seen him look so on edge.

I backpedaled. "It's nothing." I didn't want to fight with him, not about his brother, not about anything. Nate was my problem, he always had been. There was no reason for me to drive a wedge between them, that wasn't fair.

"Don't you dare shut me out. Tell me what is going on."

I bit my lip, trying to brush aside his concern. "I told you, he wants more from me and his actions are, well, they're reflecting his intentions more than ever." Every touch was lingering, every hand hold felt less friendly. His sweet kisses were getting closer and closer to my lips.

"Fuck." Jeremy ran his fingers through his dark hair, making the strands stick up. "We need to tell him."

I sucked in a gasp. "No."

"Seeing you without him knowing was one thing when he was content to be your best friend." Jeremy got up, pacing my room.

"But this, him wanting you, him touching you, demanding to be in your bed. I don't like it. Someone is going to end up hurt."

"I've already been hurt." I pointed to myself, letting him know his concerns were years too late. "I've already sacrificed what I want. I've already been put in a bad position. All the things you're afraid of have already happened to me."

"Baby, I—"

"If you tell him, he'll hold on even tighter." Tears dripped from my eyes, and I brushed them away, annoyed I couldn't control them. "He'll never choose Yale. I need him to choose Yale, Jeremy, I need him to be more than two hours away from me. He can't go to Emerson, he can't. I couldn't take it, I—"

"Shhhh." Jeremy took my face in his warm palms. "Okay. Okay, baby. I'm sorry." He kissed me, pulling me into his lap, rocking me gently. "Your sanity matters so much more than my jealousy. I hate the thought of you two spending the night together. You're not his girl. Actually, you never have been. You're mine."

I wanted that to be true. I wanted to be able to give Jeremy the relationship he deserved. That wasn't the way my world worked. That wasn't something I could offer him. Not now, and maybe not ever. All the elation I'd felt before, all the smiling and daydreaming was gone. In its place I felt hopeless and guilt ridden. The boy I loved as a friend was ruining the life I was trying to build with the boy I was in love with.

"If we want the world to keep spinning, in Nate's eyes, I'll always be his girl." I wiped my tears away before burying my face in his shirt.

"No one would survive the alternative."

Chapter Twenty-Two

Savy

Jeremy left five minutes before Nate's SUV pulled into his driveway. I wasn't sure where Jeremy went, but I knew he wasn't planning on staying home. He said it would be too hard staring at the clock, knowing that Nate and I were going to be together all night. I hated that part of me was scared he'd go out and find another girl to occupy his time. Another girl who wasn't complicated, who didn't have the baggage of his volatile baby brother hanging around her neck. Jeremy didn't put that weight on my shoulders, although up until this summer, he'd never done anything to lighten my load either. Logically, I knew until he'd left for college, he was a kid himself and wasn't equipped to handle Nate. I wasn't either, yet I'd done my best. I guess what I was trying to say was, I didn't want Jeremy to give up on me. My issues were his issues too, and I hoped that he remembered that.

"Earth to Sav." Nate waved his free hand in front of my face, the other was around my shoulders. "You okay? You spaced out."

I smiled, scooping up some more popcorn from the bowl I'd purposefully placed between us. "I'm here." I was...here. Stuck. Laid up in my bed, propped against my headboard with Nate beside me and Jeremy on my mind.

Nate moved the bowl to his lap, scooting closer to me until his hip was touching mine. Fantastic. As if my night wasn't already complicated enough, my best friend was going to try to make a move during a terrible action flick. Usually he let me pick the movie, and usually he was fine with a few feet separating us. Not tonight. Everything about this evening seemed different. I was grumpy, and distant. His arm tightened around me, his free hand coming up to my chin. I was frozen, completely unsure of what to do. Oh hell. He going to try to kiss me. How did I stop that from happening? I stopped breathing, and my heart stuttered in my chest.

"Nate? What are you—" Before I could get another word out, his lips met mine. My stomach dropped, and I pulled back, shaking my head.

"What's wrong?"

What's wrong? What wasn't wrong.

We'd never kissed on the mouth before. All these years his casual affection had become part of our relationship. Maybe I should've stopped him from holding my hand and kissing my forehead. Maybe in his mind this was a natural progression from small gestures to more obvious ones. In my mind, it was the last thing I wanted to happen.

"Nate, I'm, uh... Don't do that, okay?" Even in defending myself I wasn't assertive. I was still trying to save his feelings and his pride. I didn't want to hurt him, ever, but that was what got me into this mess in the first place.

Total irony: I could tell Jeremy anything and he was cool with it. Wanted it. He insisted I never hold back with him.

"You've never stopped me before." He didn't seem wounded, more like he was confused.

I was guessing he thought his friendly kisses and touches meant more. Which meant, when I hadn't stopped him, *I'd* done this to him, and to myself. I felt as confused as Nate looked. I was suddenly questioning every friendly interaction. "Nate, um, before, everything felt innocent."

"Oh." He's brow furrowed, like he was thinking hard. "You're not ready for that."

I shifted, putting some more distance between us. "I don't think I'll ever be ready for that." I willed the tears that were threatening to go away. I hated how sad and weak I felt and sounded. I hated that it suddenly seemed like I'd led him on. Not only was I in love with his brother, but I hadn't made it clear enough how I felt about Nate for all these years. I hung my head. "I'm sorry." I was so immensely sorry.

I was sorry that he lost his dad. Sorry I'd been charged as his watcher. I was sorry that his mom wasn't strong enough to handle him, and that she wasn't strong enough to demand he get help.

I was sorry that my parents cared more about their friend than their daughter. I was sorry that Jeremy washed his hands of his brother, moving away to college without looking back. I was sorry I fell in love with Jeremy and with the freedom he showed me.

I was sorry that Nate was hurting, I was sorry I was the cause of his pain. There were so many damn things that I was sorry for, and they were crashing into me over and over like waves of grief, suffocating me in their sadness.

"Don't be sorry." Nate wrapped me in his arms, kissing the top of my head softly. "Don't cry. Everything is going to be okay."

I sobbed, his shirt absorbing my tears.

I knew I should tell him to leave. I knew I should stop leading him on now that I saw it through his eyes.

I was selfish, the new me was a selfish stupid brat.

I needed my best friend, the way he'd needed me all these years.

I didn't make him leave. I didn't correct his assumptions.

I let him pull me under the covers and hold me while I cried myself to sleep.

Chapter Twenty-Three

Jeremy

Savy was sick. Or least that was what Nathan told me when he'd left for his evening shift at the gym. He stayed at her house last night and said she woke up with a cold. I made a silent joke about her being *sick* of him even though I didn't really think it was funny. I hated how jealous I was of my own brother. I tried to justify it by telling myself I was in love and love made you do stupid things. No one set out to hurt him, to betray him. There was no ill intent, and I kept repeating that to make myself feel better. After yesterday, seeing Savy break down at the thought of him at Emerson, I felt a little out of control. Like things were starting to spiral and head in a direction that none of us saw coming.

I pushed those thoughts aside to the icky file in my brain.

I knocked on Savy's door, deciding against the tree because it was still light outside and her parents' cars weren't in the driveway. I stepped back as the door opened, Savy was standing there in a robe. Her hair was piled on her head and she was holding a balled up tissue in her fist. I held up the chicken soup I'd had delivered to my house. "Hungry?"

She sighed and opened the door wider, letting me inside with a small shrug.

I sat the soup on the table by the door, reaching out to feel her forehead with the back of my hand. "You don't have a fever. What's going on?" I didn't care if she was contagious, I'd happily get whatever she had for a chance to spend some time with her.

"I don't know." She shuffled into the kitchen, pulling two bowls down from a glass fronted cabinet. "I cried myself to sleep, then woke up feeling like a crappy person."

"You aren't a crappy person. Why'd you cry yourself to sleep? I thought Nathan stayed the night?" I took the bowls from her, setting them on the island and opening the soup.

"He kissed me."

I dropped the spoon into the soup and watched it sink to the bottom. "Then what?" I was trying not to freak out, trying to not let my ego or pride get in the way of reason.

"I told him to stop." Savy perched on a stool. "Then I realized everything is my fault. I led him on. I let him hold my hand, hug me and kiss my temple, and I let him sleepover. To me it was our friendship, but to him it was more." She wiped at her beautiful eyes. "I did this to him. I'm going to hurt him really bad." She shook her head. "It's all my fault."

"It's not your fault, baby." I rounded the counter, putting my hands on her shoulders and rubbing them as she rested her head on my chest. "You let your friendship be whatever Nathan needed it to be. You were conditioned to give him what he needed to be okay, and so you did." I closed my eyes, silently cussing my mom and her parents. "You didn't intentionally lead him on."

"Yeah well, I intentionally slept with his brother." Her words were muffled against my shirt. "Either way you slice it, I'm a terrible friend."

"You saved his life, over and over."

"Now I'm going to ruin it." Savy shook her head back and forth. "You should go, you shouldn't be here. This isn't right, it isn't fair. Nate lives for me, he loves me and—"

"*I* love you Savy." I pushed her back, dipping down so I could meet her sad watery eyes. "I love you, and I won't apologize for that. Nathan has demanded all of you for years, he's commanded your life. Maybe we're selfish, but it's okay to be selfish sometimes. It's okay to go after the life you want. It's okay to be happy." I cupped her face, using my thumbs to wipe her cheeks. "You weren't dating my brother, you didn't cheat on him. You not wanting him to kiss you is *not* something you need to feel guilty about."

"We should tell him the truth."

"What about Emerson?"

She shook her head again. "What we're doing, it's not fair to him. He's in the dark. Even if it's misguided, he's hoping for a future with me that I'll never want." She tried to smile, but all I saw was how sad she was. "Maybe he'll go to Emerson, maybe he'll go to Yale. Either way, it's time I tell him the truth. Protecting his feelings isn't helping him anymore, and the repercussions are mine to bear."

"No." I kissed her forehead, then rested my chin against her hair. "You aren't alone anymore. Nathan isn't your sole responsibility. We'll tell him together. We'll deal with the fallout together. Then together, we'll help him heal."

***

I didn't want to say I talked my way into her bed, because that sounds a little fuck-boyish. But I didn't want to leave her when she was feeling so low. The two orgasms I'd given her seemed to improve her mood quite a bit.

"You're kind of slob, you know that right?"

The soup hadn't filled me up, so now I was eating ramen noodles out of the Styrofoam carton in the middle of the night. I took another large slurping bite, smiling around it. "I know." I held the fork full of noodle out, letting Savy have a taste of my midnight snack. "You wear out my body, baby. I need to re-fuel so I can make you come again." I winked, loving how my dirty words made her blush.

"I don't know if I can handle another one." She was trying to meet me in the middle, trying to be bolder, and it was turning me all the way on.

I gasped playfully, setting my food to the side, ignoring my fork as it fell to the carpet. "Challenge accepted, baby." I tackled her, sheathing myself with a condom before settling between her thighs.

I sank inside her warm heat, groaning at how good she felt wrapped around me. I went slow, moving in and out at an unhurried pace.

I wanted to fall asleep like this, completely connected to the girl I loved.

Chapter Twenty-Four

Jeremy

I held Savy all night. I reassured her she wasn't a bad person. Her thinking that was insane, I'd always called her a saint. Salvation. Angel. She was everything Nathan needed her to be, whenever he needed it. She was a child when he held her hand, she was naïve when he kissed her head. How could she possibly have led him on when she was so pure and innocent? It wasn't until I corrupted her that she could see what Nathan saw. It wasn't until she understood lust and want that she recognized what he desired.

We were going to talk to him today, sit him down and explain what happened over the past few weeks. We wanted him to know he was loved and wanted. He still had a brother, and he still had a best friend. We both wanted to move forward with him with no more lies between us. I hated feeling jealous of him, and I didn't want to grow to resent him and his relationship with Savy, who was overwhelmed with sadness and uncertainty when it came to Nathan, and that wasn't healthy either.

I'd been lying awake for the last few hours, rehearsing what to say in my mind. Trying to come up with the right words was proving to be difficult. Now the sun was up and I needed to go home before anyone noticed I was missing. I stretched, rolling out of Savy's bed and smiling down at her still sleeping form. She felt so badly about hurting Nathan that she'd made herself physically ill. "Baby, I've got—"

"Sav. Hey you up yet?" I froze as Savy's eyes popped open.

She flew out of bed and lunged for the door. "Nate, hold on I'm—"

She didn't make it. Nathan walked in, assessing her in my shirt before moving his gaze across the room to me. I was in my jeans. "Jeremy? What...Sav?"

I didn't want him to find out like this. Fuck. Maybe this was how Savy felt, this guilt and irritation at the pain she knew she'd cause. It seemed inevitable. We were always going to hurt him. This was always going to blow up in our faces. How stupid of us, to think we wouldn't be right where we were.

"Nathan, fuck. I know how this looks, but please stay calm and let me explain."

"Explain?" He took a step toward me, his finger jabbing close to my face. "Explain why I walked in and found you in Sav's room first thing in the morning. Why you're in my girl's room at all?"

"Nate, I'm not—"

"Savy, baby, get dressed." I held my hand out past my brother, stopping her from getting involved. I did this.

I deserved everything that was coming. He could take his hurt out on me. It was the least I could do. I abandoned my brother the moment our father died, and then I'd gone and fell in love with his best friend, his everything.

"Baby?" he growled, his neck cracking. "Why the fuck is she naked under your shirt? Why the fuck are you here?"

"We're, uh, we've been hanging out." I winced, hating how stupid that sounded. It was more than that, and not owning up to it tore at my heart. "We're together." Even that sounded shallow. I felt things for Savy. Things I'd never felt for anyone else. What started out as a favor to a girl who never got the chance to live ended up as something so much more. "I'm in love with her. I know that hurts you."

"Hurts me?"

"Jeremy, please go." Savy was still only wearing my shirt, her arms stretched out between us, the material kissing the tops of her bare thighs. "Let me talk to him, let me deal with this."

My gaze met hers, earnest and terrified. She was telling me to leave, she was giving me an out. She'd stay here. She'd calm my brother. She'd smooth the rage I saw boiling inside of him. I was wrong to think he would never hurt me. I was wrong to think that we wouldn't hurt him.

If I walked out of this room, if I left her to fix yet another Nathan tantrum, I was no better than my parents, or than hers. I wouldn't do that to her, not today and not ever again. "No, baby, I'm not going anywhere."

Nathan leapt across the room, knocking Savy down onto her bed. The sheets were still rumbled from the way I took her before the sun came up. His hands fastened around my throat, his body weight crashing on top of me until we were both on the floor of her room. "Call her baby one more time and see what happens." He slammed my head against the carpet, making me see stars. "She's not yours." Nathan swallowed, his gaze darting from me to the gorgeous terrified girl shaking beside us. "You had no right to touch her, to talk to her, to defile her. She's mine. She's always been mine." He slammed my head against the carpet again, the pain not even registering with my brain yet. "Tell him Savy, tell him you're mine."

I rolled my attention to the side, watching helplessly as tears streaked down her face, seeing the fear in her beautiful eyes. She nodded, slowly getting to her feet. "You're right Nate." Her hand cautiously reached out rubbing his arm. "I'm yours. I'm yours and I should have never let him touch me."

After everything she'd said yesterday, all the truths she wanted to tell him, she was lying to save us. I couldn't let her. If she convinced him to let me go, it would come at I price I refused to let her pay. Her freedom and her love, which was worth more to me than anything. She was fighting for me, but I would fight harder for her.

"Savy, no." I grabbed at his hands, trying to pry them from my throat. I took a deep breath, trying to clear the blurred edges of my mind. "I'm in love with her."

Nathan's hold tightened, my attempts no match for his strength fueled by anger and betrayal. We both looked over at Savy, wanting to see two very different things. He wanted to know that my emotions were one-sided, that she had a small lapse in judgment and that she would always belong to him.

I wanted to know that she heard me, that she believed my words were true, and that she knew I'd never leave her alone with her burden again.

I smiled when I saw it, Savy's answer.

And then my world went dark.

Chapter Twenty-Five

Savy

I'd called the paramedics, and made Nate go home before they turned onto our street. I tried to save the man I was in love with, and protect the friend I'd always loved. I couldn't lose them, either of them. I'd told the EMT that Jeremy fell, that he'd tripped and hit is head on my desk on his way down. I didn't know if I did the right thing. I was so used to protecting Nate, it seemed to be a habit I was unable to break.

For two days I'd been at the hospital, sitting across from Nate on opposite sides of Jeremy's hospital bed. My parents came and went all day, bringing food and clothes and coffee. Their mother slept in the recliner in the corner, the doctors had to give her medicine to help her calm down.

Jeremy had a concussion from Nate slamming his head into the ground, and he'd lost consciousness when Nate had strangled him. It'd taken me a couple of minutes to pull Nate off, to start CPR while I had the emergency operator on the phone.

The doctor said his brain function looked good, and his vitals were strong. He was healing, and they said he would wake up when he was ready.

"I'm going to the cafeteria, for coffee." Mrs. Deacon got to her feet and kissed my cheek before leaving Nate alone with me for the first time since Jeremy was admitted. She'd never asked me why Jeremy was in my room so early in the morning. Neither had my parents.

"Sav." Nate's voice sounded rough from lack of use, I hadn't heard him speak in forty eight hours. "I did this."

I glanced up, meeting his dark gaze across his brother's body. People at school made fun of Nate, they said he had a serial killer's eyes, that they held no emotion. But that wasn't true. There was plenty to see, you just had to know what to search for. Right now I could see remorse, a little fear, and love. I always saw love when I looked in Nate's eyes.

I cleared my throat, hoarse from the silent tears that never seemed to stop falling. "Yes, Nate, you did this." I reached for Jeremy's hand, squeezing it and silently prayed for him to squeeze mine back. "But I did this too. I should have been honest with you. I should have told you what was going on with Jeremy."

We had been too late. We'd come to our senses too late. I knew Nate wouldn't react well if he ever found me and Jeremy together. I knew Nate would be hurt and jealous and viciously angry. But for once in my life, I'd been selfish. I'd shoved those thoughts and their consequences to the icky file in my brain and given in to everything Jeremy offered. I'd fallen in love with the boy next door. Unfortunately for all of us, it was the wrong one.

"I hurt my brother."

I sighed, nodding slowly. "Yes, Nate, you hurt your brother." I let go of Jeremy's hand and stood, rounding the foot of his bed to stand at Nate's side. "I hurt you, and Jeremy hurt you. And then you hurt the three of us." I pointed down to Jeremy. "Jeremy will wake up." I wiped a tear off my cheek. "He will forgive you because he loves you that much." I cleared my throat and he looked up so he'd see my determination. "I will forgive you because I know I broke your heart. But Nate, if you ever touch your brother in anger again, I will walk out of your life and never ever come back. Do you understand me?"

He nodded, one small tear escaping and sliding down his cheek. I'd never seen him cry, even when their father passed away. "I won't hurt him again, I promise." He stood and wrapped his arms around me. "It's all over now."

I stiffened in his embrace. "What's all over now?" I'd learned my lesson when it came to what he was saying and what he actually meant. No more blurred lines. No more uncertainty.

"You and Jeremy." My heart was pounding as Nate's tone sounded cooler than it had moments before. "We all leave in a few weeks. Jeremy back to Northeastern and us at Emerson. It was a summer fling. You didn't mean for it to get serious." His hands started stroking my back, up and down, trying to be soothing. "It was my fault. I was working so much, leaving you all alone. Jeremy's like that. He always has a girl around. It's been that way since high school."

I made a move to back up, but Nate tightened his arms around me like a steel band. My eye's darted around the room, looking for what? A weapon? Someone to save me? For the first time in my life, I was becoming afraid of my best friend. The possessive tone of his voice, his unwavering hold on me. It didn't feel normal anymore. It didn't feel okay.

"But he'll wake up and then we'll leave." Nate leaned in, placing a lingering kiss to my cheek. "You're mine, Sav. Only ever mine."

"Nate, stop it." I pushed against his chest, but he was so damn strong I couldn't move away. "You're scaring me."

He looked at me, confused. "I'd never hurt you Sav, you know that."

"Jeremy wasn't a mistake, I'm in love with—"

"No." Nate put his palm over my mouth, his eyes growing darker than I'd ever seen them. "You don't love him. It's lust. It's a crush. It's not real. You love me. It's always been you and me." He moved his hold to my jaw, his grip tight, but not painful. "I was being patient with you, going slow. We have forever to be together, what's the rush?" His hand moved down to my neck, his thumb stroking my rapid pulse. "But you needed more, I suppose."

I was frozen in shock and fear. I was afraid, for the first time in my life to tell him no. Figured, when I was ready to put my foot down and take control of my life, he decided to lose his last thread of reality.

Part of me was angry, furious that we had caused him to snap, after all this time. He had years to try for me, years to show these cards. But he'd been happy to be my friend, or so I thought. Now, when I was ready to stand up to him, and his brother was lying helpless in a hospital bed I worried if Nate would he take my rejection out on Jeremy.

Nate's fingertips trailed along my collarbone. I felt sick, my stomach churning. "Please stop, please." I hung my head, irritated I didn't sound stronger.

"What's wrong? Isn't this what you need? This is why you're with Jeremy." Nate sounded genuinely confused.

I shook my head. "No Nate. No. This isn't why I'm with Jeremy." I put my hand on top of his. "*This*, has nothing to do with my feelings for him."

I loved Jeremy because he was sweet. Good-hearted and easy-going. He laughed and joked, and saw the brighter side of life. He loved adventure and trying new things, He didn't want shadows and confusion. He liked things straightforward. He made me feel like I was constantly basking in the warm summer sun. He pulled me out of a life I never asked for and showed me what it felt like to be free.

"He gives you things I don't." Nate's brow was furrowed, like he was trying to work a puzzle out in his mind. "I didn't know you wanted those things. You said you weren't ready. I can give them to you. I can give you everything. The whole world."

My heart was breaking for my best friend, and shattering for his older brother. We'd destroyed Nate with our love, and I couldn't find it in me to wish it all away. I'd do it over again. I'd fall in love with Jeremy a million times in a million different ways. Maybe that was selfish, but I didn't care. Nate wasn't the monster. I was. He was confused because I hadn't been strong enough to tell him how I really felt the other day. I couldn't seem to stop screwing up our lives.

"I don't want those things with you." My heart was pounding. "I love you Nate, you are my best friend. But the relationship I have with Jeremy is different."

Nate loosened his hold on my body. "Oh." His jaw was clenched as he brought his hands back to his sides. "Okay."

I backed away, cautiously. "Okay?" He nodded, his gaze on Jeremy's blankets, like he couldn't look at me. "You understand that I love you, and you're my best friend, but Jeremy is my boyfriend." I wanted to make sure that I didn't confuse him ever again.

I knew logically that some of the things I blamed myself for weren't my fault. I had been too young to be given the responsibility of managing and caring for a boy who needed professional help.

I wasn't a child anymore. I wasn't naïve, and I wasn't anyone's salvation except my own. From this moment and for the rest of forever.

He nodded again. I sat back down in my chair, and that was how we stayed, locked in a silence that neither one of us ever saw coming, for very different reasons.

Chapter Twenty-Six

Savy

Jeremy was awake. My mom told me casually over breakfast the first morning I'd spent at my house. Nate and his mother had insisted I go home and get some real sleep. Nate said he was worried about me, but I knew it was because he didn't want me around his brother. Either way, my presence, for the first time since we'd met twelve years ago, was making him agitated. Of course, his mom immediately took his side, because no one wanted an anxious Nate roaming the world.

I'd have slept better at the hospital, watching over Jeremy. I didn't get "real" sleep. I'd had nightmare after nightmare. I'd dreamt that Nate smothered his brother while he was sleeping. I'd dreamt that it was Nate in that bed instead of Jeremy. Each and every time I closed my eyes, only bad thoughts flooded up from my subconscious.

Over a giant banana nut muffin, my mother said *Oh, I forget to tell you, Jeremy woke up.* I dropped my muffin onto the cheery yellow plate and walked out the door without saying a word. I didn't have my own car, so I'd stomped across the yard, went to Jeremy's room, got the keys and took his car. I wore his sunglasses, and I rolled the windows to let the wind wreak havoc on my hair. For the first time in days, I felt like I could breathe again.

Butterflies banged their wings against my stomach as I pushed open the door to his room. I was nervous, and excited, and terrified. I couldn't wait to see him, to touch him, and hear his voice. At the same time, I was afraid of Nate's reaction, afraid of what he would do when he once again saw the love in my eyes for his brother.

I was anxious that Jeremy wouldn't be happy to see me, that he would blame me for what happened. Because no matter how much personal growth I'd tacked on in the last few days, I still couldn't help but feel like every single thing that happened was all my fault.

Jeremy was sitting up in bed, a different gown on his tanned body from when I'd been forced to leave last night. He was holding a cup of bright red Jello and his hair was a mess. When he saw me, he smiled. "Hey, baby."

My breath left my body in a rush. "Hi." My gaze left him long enough to dart around the room to see we were alone. I crossed the room and climbed into his bed, sighing with relief when he wrapped his arms around me. "I'm so sorry I wasn't here when you woke up. I'm so sorry about what happened and I—"

"Savy, baby." Jeremy put his hand on my cheeks, wiping away my tears. "None of this was your fault. I'm so fucking happy to see you. God. I love you so much." His hands moved down my arms, turning over my wrists, inspecting every inch of me he could see. "Are you okay? Did he—"

"No." I shook my head. "No, he didn't hurt me."

Now was not the time to tell Jeremy about Nate's mood yesterday, about the things he said to me. All that mattered in this moment was that Jeremy was awake, that he still loved me.

He swallowed, the action making him wince. "Does anyone know what happened?"

I dropped my gaze to my lap, shame flooding my system. It'd made so much sense while we were in the thick of it, but now, it all seemed so careless. "I told the paramedics that you fell. I, uh, Nate was so upset and I...I did what I always do, I guess. I made it better." I felt ashamed, and disgusted with myself.

My first instinct was to smooth things over, not create waves. Nate had almost killed his older brother, and I made excuses for him. "I'm sorry, my god, I should have told them what I happened. I should have said something."

Jeremy shook his head, his hand coming to my cheek again. "No, baby, you did the right thing."

"Did I?" I scoffed. "Nate needs help. He's always needed help. He's getting worse. He *hurt* you."

"You're right, Nathan needs help. But getting arrested and going to prison would not put him on the right track." Jeremy laid back against the scratchy white pillow, pulling me against his chest. "Besides, Nathan's reaction was warranted. In his mind, his brother stole his girl." Jeremy kissed the top of my head. "I'd have kicked my ass too."

I snorted, slapping his chest lightly. "Don't make jokes."

"I'm not." I could hear the smile in is hoarse voice.

I pulled back so I could see the humor in his eyes. "You've been in a coma for three days."

"I needed to rest a bit."

I rolled my eyes. "You had a concussion. You could've died. Nate could've killed you." I shook my head, my eyes filling with tears all over again. "I swear, never in a million years did I think he would harm you. I knew when he found out he'd be angry. I knew it would hurt him." Jeremy wiped my cheeks with his thumbs, love shinning in his gaze. "I was so selfish, and it almost got you killed."

"Hey, now, that's enough of that." He held my face so gently like I was made of something precious. "Don't backtrack on me now, baby. Living your life isn't being selfish. It's just living." He leaned forward and kissed my lips for the first time in what felt like forever. I'd missed him. I'd missed every single thing about him. "We fucked up, but we'll make it right." He kissed me again, stealing all thoughts.

Nothing else existed when I was wrapped in Jeremy's arms, drunk from his mouth on mine. All too soon the hospital door opened and we jerked apart. Nate and their mother were back. I turned to face the wall, taking deep breaths to try and calm my racing heart. I was probably blushing too. That was the last thing Nate needed to see right now, his brother and I locked together.

"Oh, Savy, sweetheart, I didn't know you were here." Mrs. Deacon carried a bouquet of flowers into the room and sat them on the windowsill, bright yellow daisies and blue hydrangea. "I called your mother this morning and let her know we'd get to bring Jeremy home tomorrow."

"She told me." I smiled and slipped off Jeremy's bed with my hands tucked behind my back. I wanted to stay next to him. I wanted to handcuff him to me so I could touch him constantly. But Nate was watching us, his eyes narrowed. "I thought I'd come see for myself that Jeremy was okay."

"You're so sweet to love my boys the way you do."

I glanced at Jeremy and he winked, making heat start to creep over my cheeks all over again. His mom wasn't wrong. I did love her boys. If she knew the mess we were in, she probably wouldn't be cheerfully fluffing flowers.

"Come on, Sav. I'll drive you home." Nate pushed away from the wall he'd been leaning on, completely ignoring his brother. "You don't need to sit here all day."

Of course I didn't *need* to, but I wanted to. I wanted to stay with Jeremy until he was released, and then I wanted to drive him home and tuck him into bed. I wanted to watch him breathe. I wanted to sleep in his arms. But. The best thing for everyone involved was for me to let Nate take me home. It'd keep him away from his brother. Maybe we could start to rebuild our friendship.

"No." Jeremy crossed his arms over his chest, his gaze trained on Nate. "You should both stay. We can watch a movie. I need the company."

Nate's jaw clenched. My stomach rolled at the tension between them. And their mom kept on fluffing those stupid fucking flowers. I wanted to scream. I wanted to demand she wake up and realize there was a storm brewing right in front of her face.

Nate glared at his older brother. "One movie." He grabbed the recliner his mom had been using the last couple of days and moved it away from the hospital bed. "Here Savy." He pulled his chair next to mine, both of us more than a few feet away from Jeremy. His point was made, he was still pissed, and he was in charge.

"Well since you two are here, I'm going to run to the grocery store." Mrs. Deacon moved Jeremy's dark hair and placed a kiss on his forehead. "I want you to have all your favorite things to eat at home."

"Thanks mom." Jeremy smiled until the door shut behind her, then turned to his brother. "Leave."

"Are you high?" Nate didn't joke, he was honestly asking if Jeremy was high. I was a little curious myself. I'd never heard him openly try to piss off his brother before, especially when it came to me.

No one had ever demanded to be alone with me. No one had ever demanded Nate give me up.

"Leave, or I call the doctors in here and tell them what really happened in Savy's bedroom." Jeremy crossed his arms over his chest, his chin raised. He wasn't backing down and he wasn't bluffing.

I glanced over at Nate, then back to Jeremy. I was sitting between them, and the metaphor wasn't lost on me. I loved them both, but I was in love with only one of them.

Nate was standing, straight as a board, his whole body tensed and ready to coil. "You get one hour, and then I'm coming to take Sav home. You push me, I tell her parents I caught you fucking her."

I flinched at his words. I'd never heard Nate speak like that about me, so callous and cold. I was the one person in the world that he cared about, that he was soft and careful with. Twelve years friendship. No. More than friendship. Twelve years of me taking care of Nate. Bending and yielding to Nate. Turning my life inside out for Nate, and he'd shit on me to keep Jeremy away.

I didn't care if he told my parents. I was eighteen and weeks away from starting college.

Nate had changed the playing field, and I didn't think he'd like my new rules.

Chapter Twenty-Seven

Jeremy

I was alive, I was awake, and I had Savy lying in my arms. I knew my world was fucked, but at the moment, I didn't care. I didn't care Nathan was hurt. I didn't care he was pissed. I'd have done it all over again, every single thing, if it meant that I'd end up with Savannah. Sure, if I'd told Nathan the truth when it all started and deal with the fallout then, before he caught her wearing my shirt at seven o'clock in the morning, that would've been a better approach. It didn't change how I felt. I'd never give her up.

I'd known Savannah Nightingale for most of her life. Yeah, I was a fucking idiot for not realizing how spectacular she was until this summer. The girl next door, my brother's savior, my only love. I was consumed with every single thing about her. Her long silky hair, and the way she blushed so easily. The way she sang along to the radio, and the way she looked in the moonlight. The way she kissed and the sounds she made when she came apart in my arms. I was in love with every moment we'd spent together. I'd do everything in my power to make sure she was mine forever.

We were young, I knew that. She needed to go to college, and I needed to finish my degree. But there would never be another girl for me. We'd lived a lot in our short years, endured even more. She'd spent years as Nathan's keeper, and I'd spent my whole life until I went to college avoiding saying or doing anything to upset him. We've both been trapped by his moods and whims. Now we were free, and I refused to go back to the way it was before.

I forgave my brother for knocking me out. I'd have done the same thing if I thought I lost Savy. Strangling me was a little much.

But that was Nathan. Prison wasn't were he belonged, it wouldn't do him or society any good. He needed help, real professional help. Although I wouldn't call the police, I had every intention of telling my mom the truth. Savy's parents too. They needed to know that Nathan wasn't good for her. How they didn't see that was unfuckingbelievable. They all needed to understand that she couldn't and shouldn't be in charge of him anymore.

I didn't think he'd physically hurt her, but her sanity and her soul were at stake, and doing any more damage to her sense of self was unacceptable.

"What are you thinking about?" She turned on her side, smiling up at me. "You've been quiet. Are you feeling okay?"

"I'm perfect." I kissed her lips, swiping my tongue against the seam. "I'm ready to get out of here. Ready for this summer to be over." Her expression fell, her eyes darting to the crisp white sheets between us. I put my finger under her chin, lifting her gaze back to mine. "I'm ready to move back to school. I'm ready for you to move too. I want weekends alone with you. I want date nights and Facetime calls. I want to be with you, away from everything here that tried to keep us apart."

She bit at her lower lip, her eyes filling with tears. "Nate told me was going to Emerson." She wiped them away, like they made her angry. "I should switch schools. I should go to Yale. By the time he realizes what I've done, it'll be too late."

"No." I renewed a vow I'd made to myself mere minutes ago. Nathan wouldn't control her life anymore. I was not about to let him push Savy away from me, and away from what she wanted for her future. "You're going to Emerson." I licked my lips, staring at the door to make sure he wasn't out there spying on us. "I'm going to talk to my mom, and I'm going to talk to your parents. I'll tell them what happened. I'll tell them why it happened. It's time. They need to know. Nathan needs help, and you need to be far away from him."

Savy's gaze darted to the door, clearly wary as I was. "You think it'll work? You think they'll help?"

I couldn't blame her for having no faith in the three parents we had between us. They'd never helped her before. They'd never stepped in and put a stop to Nathan's overbearing friendship. They were more than happy to let her do all the dirty work.

"Honestly, I don't know." I hated saying that to her, I hated that it was the truth. I didn't know for sure if my mom would rise to the occasion and get Nathan to the right doctors. I didn't know if Savy's parents would help her. I didn't know if they'd be pissed that I upset the precarious balance they'd established at the expense of a sweet girl.

All I knew was that I told Savy I'd help her be free, and I wasn't going to let her down.

I cupped her beautiful face. "You and I, we're a team. We're going to figure this out, baby. You're going to Emerson, and I'm going back to Northeastern. I'm going to take you on corny dates, and I'm going to fuck you in your tiny dorm room. Everything is going to be all right."

"I love you." Her face lit up as she spoke those words. "You said it before everything went bad, and I wanted you to know, I love you too." I kissed her lips, groaning when she opened for me.

I wanted to get out of here. I wanted to be back in her bedroom, the door locked and our whispers as quiet as possible. I wanted to hold her, really hold her.

"Sav." Nathan was standing in the open doorway, backlit from the fluorescents in the hallway. His jaw was clenched tight, his hands in fists at his sides, his gaze as dark as it'd been when he was choking me a few days ago. He was pissed all over again. He didn't like me touching her, and he didn't like me kissing her for fucking sure. "Let's go." He was barely controlling his desire to pounce on me, and it seemed as though it was taking all the strength he possessed to keep his shit in check.

Savy leaned forward, her lips brushing against the shell of my ear. "I told him if he ever hurt you again, I would never speak to him again."

Well that explained the contained rage swimming in his eyes. "Don't go. It's not worth it, baby. We'll figure this out—"

"Sav, now." He held out his hand, like he was waiting for a child to obey his command. "Let's go."

I didn't want her leave, especially with him. I didn't think he'd hurt her, but that didn't mean that I wanted her alone with him. He'd crossed a line, and he needed help. He'd always been unpredictable, and given to extreme behavior, but now? He was off the hook. His reactions to other people were known, if not acceptable, but this was the first time he'd gone after someone he loved.

"It's okay." She kissed my cheek, speaking softly so only I could hear. "There's nothing we can do to help him with you lying in a hospital bed. Get some rest and we'll figure everything out once you're home."

I nodded. My heart physically aching as she climbed off my bed and followed my brother out the door, once again, sacrificing herself.

Chapter Twenty-Eight

Jeremy

I hated Savy left with Nathan. I hated she wasn't lying here next to me. I wanted her to stay. To sleep in my arms where I could keep her safe and sane. She'd made a good point though, my being in this bed useless wasn't going to help Nathan. I needed to heal, and I needed to talk to our parents. I needed strength for the discussions that should've been had years ago. I lay my head back and grinned. My pillow still smelled like Savy's sweet scent.

"Hey man, you good for a visit?" Max poked his head into the open doorway, a smile on his face.

I waved him inside. "I'm betting you can't wait to say 'I told you so.'"

"The 'I told you so' is implied." He pulled the guest chair closer to my bedside. "What the fuck happened, bro?"

I sighed, studying one of my oldest friends, glad he was here. "Nathan walked in on me and Savy."

"He caught you two..." He made a lewd motion with his hand.

"Morning after, but it was obvious what'd happened between us."

"He went nuts, attacked you and put you into a coma." He shook his head. "How is he still walking around? How is he not behind bars right now? He fucking *attacked* you."

No shit. I'd never forget it as long as I lived. "He's my brother. He needs help. He doesn't belong in prison. Savy told the EMT I fell, and when the cops questioned me I told them the same thing."

"You were in a coma for almost three days."

I shrugged knowing nothing I said could make this sound all right. "The docs said that was more emotional healing than physical." Apparently having your brother try to kill you fucked with your brain on many levels.

Max scoffed. "You sound as crazy as he acts, you know that, right?" I nodded. "You're in love with her?"

"Head over heels, man."

"Why now?"

Valid, but irrelevant at this point. "For the first time, I saw her for who she is. I *saw* her. She was drowning. Losing her soul under the weight of all thing Nathan, which was partly my fault."

"You feel like you owe her? Is that it?"

"No." I shook my head. "It has nothing to do with owing her. She makes me want to be a man worth her love. There's so much goodness in her, so much light. I want her to live in that light."

"I get that," Max said. "Who wouldn't want that for the girl they love."

The nurse stepped in, setting a pitcher of water and a small cup on my tray. "Visiting hours are almost over." She smiled at Max and he winked at her as she left.

"You really going to make a move on my nurse?" I laughed, waving him away. "Get out of here, man. I need my rest."

He stood, clapping his hand with mine. "I'm happy for you and Savy. I really am."

"Thanks, bro." It felt good having someone rooting for us who was on our side and wanted to see us make it. "Come by the house before you head back to the west coast."

"You know it." He rubbed his palms together. "I'm going to go see what time that cute little nurse gets off." He winked on his way out the door making me chuckle.

I rested against my pillows glad he'd stopped by. Sometimes having an old friend was a giant pain in the ass, but most times, it was exactly what I needed.

Chapter Twenty-Nine

Savy

My parents weren't home when Nate and I made it back to my house. They'd texted to let me know they were taking Mrs. Deacon to dinner, to help her decompress from the last few *trying* days. If only they knew the truth, they wouldn't be out celebrating Jeremy's recovery.

The worst was yet to come. Jeremy wanted to have Nate committed, and after what I'd witness in my bedroom, I agreed it was time. It'd taken everything in me to get him to let go of his brother's neck, to stop slamming his head into the floor. Then, the way he reacted with me at the hospital yesterday, I was pretty sure was the first time he'd flipped his switch with me.

Nate was livid, catching me and Jeremy together, knowing that we'd been intimate. He hated that Jeremy loved me, and he hated even more that I loved him back. I couldn't blame Nate for his feelings, but I could for his actions. Nate understood right from wrong, I knew he did. He understood rules and the things that could get him into trouble. He simply didn't care.

He'd been quiet on the drive home from the hospital. He wasn't being rude, or cruel. Pensive, and intense. Which was more terrifying. He'd been irritated when he dragged me out of Jeremy's room, and I expected him to have more questions. Instead, I was met with silence and that made my nervous about what he was thinking.

I was exhausted and I needed some space. "I'm going to bed." I left him by the front door, thinking it was clear that he needed to let himself out as I headed up the stairs. But when I opened my bedroom door, I realized that he was behind me. He'd silently followed me to my room. "What are you doing Nate? Go home."

I was getting stronger every day, voicing my wants and opinions. I couldn't help but wonder who would the two of us be if I'd started to do this years ago. Would Jeremy have even felt the need to liberate me? No. I wouldn't have needed help in the attic. I wouldn't've been swimming in the Deacon's pool with desperation pulsing off of me. Maybe I'd have Jeremy in my life, maybe Nate would have received the help he needed. All the speculation in the world didn't change where we were now. There was no way to know the outcome of what ifs, and time travel didn't exist. These were the cards that were dealt, the cards I'd held in my hand for so long. This was our life, but it wasn't going to be anymore.

He shook his head slowly, shutting the door behind him and throwing the lock. "No, I'm going to stay."

I wrapped my arms around my body, fighting off the chill his tone engendered. I'd heard him use that disconnected pitch with other people, but never with me, never before. "I don't want you to stay." I pushed strength in my voice and lifted my chin. "Please, get out."

"I told you, I can give you what you want." He stepped closer, crowding my space, making me back away until I had nowhere else to go but out the window. "You said that you weren't ready, but I saw you with my brother and you lied. You are ready. I wanted to go slow. I wanted to be what you wanted me to be. But now that I know what you want, I can give you those things too."

I bit my cheek. "I don't want those things with you Nate." I hated to hurt him, to reject him like that again, but he wasn't leaving me another option. "You're my best friend, but that's all. Nothing more."

His head cocked to the side like he was a little confused. "What's Jeremy to you?"

Everything. "He's my boyfriend."

"How long have you been lying to me?" That tone, I didn't like it. I felt like he was removing himself from me, taking all the love he had for me and stripping it away. I was sure he thought I deserved it for deceiving him.

My thoughts were all over the place: guilt and remorse, fear and newfound strength. I was a mess of emotions and feelings. I'd hurt him, and I was conditioned to sooth him, to placate and not make waves. That was the past. No more lies, even if we drowned in the fallout.

"I've been seeing Jeremy since the night he helped me in the attic." I took a deep breath, gathering courage. "We started spending time together as friends, and it developed into something more. We were going to tell you the morning you walked in and found us. We didn't want to hurt you, but we both knew you weren't going to take it well. We were cowards for too long. For that, and only that, I am sorry."

Nate reached down, picking up the baseball he'd left with me all those years ago, and then hurled it across the room shattering the mirror above my dresser. I flinched as broken glass showered the framed pictures of us that lined the top.

I needed to get out of here, I knew that now. I never should've gone upstairs without insisting he leave and locking the front door. There weren't enough apologies in the world that would fix this.

The Nate I'd known all my life had retreated inside himself the moment he'd seen me with his brother. The Nate standing before me was who everyone else got. The violent unpredictable Nate, the one who didn't care who he wounded. The one who could never think past his anger. I hadn't recognized it before because I didn't want to. I didn't want to believe that my love for Jeremy had broken his brother so completely.

I stepped forward, moving to shove past him and out the door. I was already racing for the front door and dialing the police in my mind. Instead of the break for freedom I'd envisioned, Nate grabbed my arm and tossed me like a ragdoll onto my bed. He pinned me down, his hands yanking my wrists above my head. His eyes were black, there was nothing left of the boy I'd saved over and over again. The boy I'd sacrificed my entire childhood for.

My Nate was gone.

I didn't plead with him to let me go. I knew he wouldn't. I stayed as calm as possible, waiting to see what his plan was, waiting to see how far he'd take this.

He moved both my wrist to one strong grip, using his other hand to caress my face. "I loved you."

Tears silently streamed down my face. "I love you too Nate. I do. I swear." I'd spent my whole life living for him, trying to be who he needed.

"Not like you love Jeremy," he stated. It didn't warrant an answer. He sure as hell wouldn't like what I was going to say. "You don't know how good we could be together, Sav." His hand trailed farther down, gripping my throat briefly before moved to my breast. "Let me show you. Let me show you how happy I can make you."

I closed my eyes, more tears leaking out the sides. My parents weren't home, Jeremy was still in the hospital, and my cell phone was on the dresser, covered in tiny shards of sharp glass. After I'd vowed to save myself, I needed someone to save me from what I knew was going to happen. "Please don't do this, Nate. Please."

He shook his head, like he was sad. "You've left me no choice. Don't you see that?" He moved his attention to my other breast, rubbing his thumb over my nipple. "You'll see, Sav. You'll see how good I can make you feel. Then you'll love me more than you love him." He placed a kiss to my lips, making me whimper. "I'm all you'll ever need. I'm all you've ever needed. You'll see."

I turned my head to the side, searching my room for anything that might help me. A fork. There was a fork from the last time Jeremy ate in here. I silently thanked him for being such a slob. Nate was distracted, both his hands roaming over my body, his lips at my neck. I stretched my arms out, coming up a few inches short. I shifted underneath him, trying to close the distance to the only weapon I could see.

He took that as an invitation. He ripped my yoga pants, then my panties. It hurt, my flesh burned where the material had pulled. But it'd given me another inch. I was crying hard. There would be no coming back from this. I couldn't explain this away. I couldn't give him yet another free pass. Nate was about to cross a line I never in a million years imagined that he'd cross.

I was losing a piece of myself, and I was losing my best friend.

His fingers trailed over my hip, skating across my stomach and between my legs. I wasn't ready for him, so he licked his hand, making bile rise up my throat. "Don't cry, Sav, everything is going to be okay." He rested his forehead against mine, his breaths coming out in ragged pants as he ruined us. "See Sav, see? I can be what you need too."

I clenched my teeth, trying not to throw up on us both. I stretched my arm out, flexing my fingers and doing everything I could to ignore the way he was touching me, violating me. His lips met mine, his kiss hard and painful. I clamped my mouth shut, refusing to give him that when he was already taking too much. He didn't seem to mind, instead he placed kisses along my neck, across my breasts, down my stomach. I let my head fall back, allowing myself a moment to cry and silently beg for all of this to stop. When his mouth closed over my clit, I took my opening and jack knifed up, grabbing the fork and slamming it into his side with a shout.

He jerked back, shocked, and reached for it.

I scrambled to my feet, tripping over my pants in a mad dash to the bedroom door. I could hear him behind me, calling my name, his footfall pounding so close. I raced down the stairs, throwing open the front door. Before I could take a step into the sunshine, I was hauled backward by my hair. My scalp screamed, a sob escaping from my throat.

"Why did you do that? I'm trying to help you. Why won't you let me love you?" He slammed me against the wall, yelling in my face. His eyes were black, the way they were when he'd attacked Jeremy.

Jeremy. He forgave his brother, even after he tried to kill him. Now, he would lose him to the instability that'd plagued Nate his whole life.

Nate's hand was once again wrapped around my throat, his lips at my ear, whispering how much he wanted me, how much he loved me, how happy we'd be forever.

I threw my arms out, once again searching for anything within my reach to stop him. He was undoing his pants button, trying to push them down with his free hand. A vase. There was an ugly vase on the small table by the door, it was full of fake flowers that my dad hated. I could feel it with my fingertips, it was so close. Nate was rubbing himself against my center, trying to gain entry. My body didn't want him. He growled, hiking up my thigh, giving me the purchase I needed. I grabbed the vase, slamming it into his head, throwing him off balance.

I clawed at the door handle, fumbling with the lock and throwing it open once again. I stumbled outside, crossing the lawn, screaming for help as tears streamed down my cheeks. I didn't have my phone, Jeremy's keys were on my bedside table. Nate was yelling my name, blood dripping down his ear and onto my dad's perfect green lawn. I'd hurt him, he was moving slow. I had nowhere to go, no one to run to. He was stronger than me, even injured, he'd overpower me. I fell to the ground when he hooked my ankle, landing so hard I lost my breath. He flipped me over, hovering above me.

"When will you learn, Sav? I'm the only person you'll ever need." He slapped me, my cheek stinging. He wasn't using his full strength though, if he had, I'd be out cold. In his mind, he wasn't hurting me, he never wanted to hurt me. Nate loved me, the only way he knew how.

Wait. That was it. He loved me the way he knew how, and I needed to meet him there.

"You're right." I took a deep inhale, trying to make my tone soothing, the way I'd called him back from the edge a hundred times before. "You're the only one for me, you're all I'll ever need Nate." I reached up, cupping his cheek. "But it can't be like this, out in the open, in the front yard? You want better for me, for us, right? I deserve better."

His gaze softened. "Of course you do, Sav." He stood, pulling me to my feet, his knuckles grazing the bruise I was sure was forming on my face. "You deserve the world, but you keep fighting me."

I nodded, like I was agreeing with him. "I've been crying, and you're mad." I dropped my eyes to my feet, like I was feeling shy. "I want a do over. I want to look nice for you. I want it to be special, don't you?"

He smiled, so tragically beautiful. "Yes."

I took another deep breath, trying to keep the hope blooming in my chest at bay. "I'm going to shower, put on something nice." I gestured to his house. "You too. Wear that blue shirt I got you last year for your birthday, okay?"

His eyes narrowed, a frown on his lips. "No." He shook his head, manically. "I love you Sav, but I don't trust you. Not after what you did with my brother." I forced my molars together, trying to keep from sobbing. "I'll wait for you, in your room. Then we'll try over again, okay?"

I swallowed past the lump in my throat. "Okay, sure." I had to take what I could get. I headed back into my house, praying like hell that my parents would come home. That Nate's mom would come home. I needed a parent. I needed someone to finally step up and check on me. To make sure I was okay. I'd bought myself time, but not space.

He followed me inside, his hand on my shoulder stopping me before I could go upstairs. "How about some tea?" I turned to study him, almost afraid he was joking. He had blood on his head, his shirt was soaked deep red where I'd stabbed him with a fork.

Nate looked like he'd been in a battle. "Sure. That'd be great." I smiled, small and thankful. "Bring it up to me? I'll leave the bathroom door unlocked."

He grinned at that, like I'd granted his wish. I was trusting him, I was leaving a door unlocked, I was asking him to take care of me. He thought he was winning. When really I was deceiving him one final time. I moved up the stairs, slowly, refusing to rush and alert him to the mistake he'd made. I didn't even close my bedroom door. I plucked my cell off the table, heading into the bathroom and turning on the shower before dialing 9-1-1.

What was my emergency the operator asked. Where did I start? I relayed my address, I let them know that there was someone inside with me, attacking me. I told them the front door was unlocked, I told them where my room was. Then I hung up, hiding my cell phone in a drawer. I climbed into the shower, curling into a ball and letting the hot water scald my skin. When I heard sirens in the background, I closed my eyes, sobbing over all that was about to happen.

Chapter Thirty

Jeremy

My mom had dinner with Savy's parents, and then they dropped her off at the hospital to visit with me. I was ready to tell her what really happened, tell her that Nathan needed to go away for a while, but before I got my chance, her phone rang. Her face went pale while she listened to whoever was on the other end of the line. My stomach sank to the floor, knowing that something terrible had happened. Her face, that was the way she'd reacted when she got the news my father had died. Someone was dead. Her phone fell from her hand, crashing to the linoleum.

"Mom?" I was too afraid to ask her what happened, too afraid of what her answer might be.

She closed her eyes, her hand going to her heart. "It's your brother. He's been arrested."

He finally snapped. After all this time because Savy wasn't there to keep him stable. I knew that would happen eventually, which was why I'd been planning on speaking with my mother tonight about getting him some real inpatient help. "Mom, this has been—"

"He attacked Savy."

Time stopped. I could feel every beat of my heart, hear every drip of my IV. I'd hurt my brother and he'd taken it out on the one person I never thought he would.

I threw my legs over the side of the bed, ripping out my IV with a wince. "Is she okay? Is she hurt? Where is she? Mom." Her gaze jerked to mine, she seemed to be in shock. "Mom."

"She's here. She's at the hospital getting checked out."

I scrambled around the room, pulling clothes from the bag my mom had brought for my discharge tomorrow. Blood was dripping from my arm and my head was pounding, but the only thing that mattered was getting to Savy.

"Jeremy. Where are you going? We need to go get your brother, we need to get him out of jail he doesn't belong there, he isn't a crim—"

"Yes, he is." I yelled and she flinched. "He attacked the one person on this planet that he actually fucking loves. He's dangerous. He's unstable. He's uncontrollable." I tugged on my shoes. "You go get him, but I'm going to Savy."

"You did this, you and her." My mom's whispered words stopped me in my tracks. "You think I didn't notice? Sneaking out and running across the yard. Coming home late. I saw you with her." She sounded disgusted. "I can't believe that you two would do that to Nathan, would push him like that."

"Push him?" My mother was either delusional or in denial, but either way it was time she was set straight. I'd planned to sit her down, have a rational and calm conversation. Unfortunately, like what happened with Nathan a few mornings ago, I was too late. "It is not my job to make life livable for my brother. It's not Savy's job to smooth every bump in his road. We are not his parents. We are not responsible for him. You are," I told her through gritted teeth as on my way out the door. "The day Dad died, you handed Nathan over to Savy. That was wrong. You and Savy's parents were wrong. You rested the weight of the world on a little girl's shoulders. Everything that's happened since, everything that's happening now, is *your* fault."

I didn't wait to hear her reply, and it didn't matter. She'd step up or she wouldn't, but either way Nathan was in police custody and he was staying there until our mother went to get him out. I wasn't running to his rescue. I forgave him for hurting me, putting me in the hospital. I couldn't forgive him for harming Savy. Never.

I went down to the main lobby, asking for Savannah Nightingale and lying to the nurses, telling them I was her brother. When I got to her room, her mom was outside the door crying, her dad was pacing up and down the hallway. When they saw me they rushed forward, both talking at once.

"Why would Nathan do this?"

"Do you know what happened?"

I held up my hands, trying my best to calm them down enough so that I could answer their questions when all I really wanted to do was shove past them and go to Savy. "I don't know what happened after Nathan took her home this afternoon, I haven't spoken to her or my brother."

"Why did he do this? He loves her." Her mom was wiping at her cheeks, almost like she was bewildered that her tears continued to flow. "Why Jeremy? Why?"

Should I tell them it was because he loved her too much? Should I tell them it was because of me, because I fell for her? Or should I tell them this happened because they never thought to ask their daughter how she felt or what she wanted? None of those answers would help them right now. I knew that. So instead I left them standing in the hallway with their questions and then locked Savy's hospital room door after I slipped inside.

She was sitting up in bed, a gown on her small frame and a bruise on her cheek. Her hair was a tangle of blonde silk and her lips were puffy and red. "Baby." I crossed the room and wrapped her in my arms, holding her as she sobbed against my chest. "Are you okay? Did he...? Tell me what happened."

"He followed me up to my room." Her voice was soft, her grip on my arms tight. "He told me that he could give me the same things you could, that he could make me feel good too."

I clenched my jaw, trying to control my rapid heartrate. She didn't need another man in her life to lose it. She needed me to hold her and listen, so I would. Even though every fiber in my being wanted to go find my brother and kick his ass.

"He t-t-touched me, but I stabbed him with a fork and he chased me when I ran. He had me up against the door, but then I hit him with a vase." She stopped, taking a deep breath. "He tackled me in the yard and told me he loved me. That's when I got him to calm down a bit, he let me go inside to shower and I called the police."

"Baby, my god, I'm so—"

"I hid in the shower, but I could hear everything. I heard the cops come in. I heard how shocked he was, then how angry. Then he was scared and he was calling my name, begging me to come tell them that we were in love." She broke down, sobs wracking her body.

I stroked her back, and held her. I told her over and over again how much I loved her, how I would never leave her again.

I told her how strong she was, how smart.

I rocked her long after she fell asleep in my arms.

Chapter Thirty-One

Savy

I woke up in yet another hospital room, but this time I was in the bed and Jeremy was sitting in an uncomfortable chair beside me. He was asleep, his arms folded across his chest and the bruising still around his neck from where Nate had choked him. The past few days felt like a nightmare, like a bad dream rolling on repeat. I'd hurt my best friend. Then he'd retaliated by almost killing his brother. He snapped when he realized I wasn't his the way he wanted me to be, and he violated me, and nearly raped me.

All because I wanted to be free, and in the process I fell in love.

"Savannah, darling, you're awake." My mom rushed over to my side, brushing the hair off my forehead. "Do you need me to call the nurse?"

"No." I shook my head while reaching for the cup of water she held out. My mouth was dry, and my throat was scratchy. I took inventory of my body, noticing that my joints were sore and everything felt stiff like I'd been asleep for days instead of hours. "Where is Dad?" I knew both my parents were in the hallway when Jeremy came in, I saw them when he opened the door.

"He went home to get you a change of clothes." She fussed with my blankets. "They said the clothes you came in wearing were torn and wet." Her gaze slowly met mine, a frown on her lips. "Did Nathan, um, what happened?" She glanced at Jeremy who was still asleep or was pretending to be to give my mother a moment. "Jeremy wouldn't tell us anything, he said it was a long story and all that mattered was letting you rest."

"Jeremy and I, we started hanging out this summer, and we fell in love." I couldn't help but smile as I said those words, even though the chain of events since Nate discovered us together were disastrous. "Nate found out, and he attacked Jeremy. That was the real reason he was in the hospital. Then, when I told Nate I didn't want a physical relationship with him, he tried to force one." I wasn't sure why I was speaking so calmly about something so horrifying, maybe all my emotions were spent. More likely, I was in shock.

"Nathan has never hurt you before, right? This isn't something that's been happening behind our backs for years?"

"No, Nate has never touched me out of anger before, not like that." I licked my lips, they felt bruised and cracked which gave me flashbacks of how roughly he'd kissed me. "Nate wanted more from me, he thought we were *more* than best friends."

"But you're in love with Jeremy?"

"I am." I glanced over to him, but he seemed relaxed and asleep. "Even if I wasn't, I still wouldn't want to be with Nate, not like that." This was the moment I came clean and spoke my truth, and it was long overdue. "When Nate and I met, we were kids, happy to be playing together, but after Mr. Deacon passed everything changed."

"Well of course it did sweetheart, he lost his father."

I scoffed. "No, that's not what's going to happen anymore. No one is going to justify Nate's behavior. No one is going to justify making a young girl responsible for a mentally unstable boy. There is no reason good enough for Nate becoming mine to look after, mine to soothe. Don't you see that?" I shook my head, irritated. "His father was gone, but his mother wasn't. She put me in an impossible position, and you and Dad let her."

"He was your best friend, you seemed so happy together." My mom's face crumbled, tears streaming down her cheeks. "We didn't know you weren't happy. We didn't know you were struggling. How would we?"

"You could've asked me." I could have told them too. I could have opened my mouth and shared my feelings and my struggles with my parents. I knew they loved me. So why hadn't I? Perhaps I too afraid that they would brush my concerns under the proverbial rug. Really, I thought it was after years of conditioning, years of life with Nate, I was afraid to live without my jailer.

My mom grabbed my hands, holding them against her cheeks and sobbing that she was sorry, that what happened to me was all her fault, that she was a terrible mother. This happened to me, yet she was making me feel guilty for being angry at her lack of involvement in my life. She was a parent. How she didn't see Nate was unstable was beyond me.

Everything except how I felt about Jeremy was completely messed up. As always, I hated that my mom was hurting. I hugged her, and told her that everything would be okay, that I was safe. Once again, I was taking care of someone else's needs ahead of my own. I had to work on not doing that.

I got her calmed down and convinced her to go find me something to eat that wasn't hospital food. She left the room, still wiping tears from her swollen eyes.

The second the door closed, Jeremy asked, "You okay?" He came over and perched on the side of my bed, cupping my bruised cheek. I was covered in bruises. Some I could explain and some I couldn't. I remembered everything, but as a whole, not in its component parts.

"I knew you were awake." I shook my head. "Who could sleep through that?" My mom and I were long overdue for that talk. She'd left me and Nate alone, not wanting to step in and be a parent.

"I pretty much went off on my mom about the same shit too." He climbed further in, wrapping his arm around my shoulders. "Rough day for parents, huh?"

"Well they've coasted for the last twelve years, so I don't feel too bad for them." I rested my head against his shoulder, feeling exhausted all over again after that "discussion" with my mom. Today had been a really long day, and I was ready for it to be over. "Can we sleep now? For real?"

He kissed the top of my head, settling us in deeper under the thin covers. "Dream of me and all the adventures we're going to have as soon as I can spring you from this hospital."

"Deal."

I'd almost drifted off, my limbs and eyelids feeling heavy, when Jeremy's whisper danced across the silence. "I love you, wild one."

Chapter Thirty-Two

Jeremy

Savy was out of the hospital and riding shotgun in my car. It'd been four weeks since everything had gone to shit with my brother. She'd refused to press charges on the stipulation that Nathan be sent to an inpatient facility for no less than one year. She told my mom she loved him, and she wanted him to find peace. My mother agreed immediately. After that Savy, told the cops she wouldn't press charges, and she refused to testify against him. Without her as a witness, the DA wasn't going to pursue the case. Savy had once again saved my brother.

Mom was contrite and apologetic. All our parents were. They saw how wrong they'd been to leave Savy and Nathan on their own, letting them deal with adult problems when they were children. There was irreparable damage done, but the future no longer looked so bleak.

Savy was moving into her dorm room at Emerson next week and was going to start seeing a therapist once a week. She needed to get over her trauma, and she needed to explore why she allowed herself to get so lost that Nathan became her whole world.

I was getting my own place near Northeastern with a couple of my buddies from the track team. Savy and I were still entirely in love. I was looking forward to the coming school year with my girl. We'd be away from our parents, and away from Nathan. We'd both be free to be exactly who we wanted. If Savy wanted to rush a sorority and party her nights away, then I'd be right by her side cheering her on. I still wanted her to do what made her happy. I hoped I'd always be one of those things.

We were too young to talk about forever, but that didn't mean that I didn't think about it, didn't wish for it. Savy had spent her whole life tied to a guy, I figured she deserved all the freedom she could handle before she tied herself to another one.

She forgave our parents, she forgave Nathan, and, I hoped, with the help of the therapist, she'd eventually forgive herself. That was the big one. The most important. Even after Nathan had attacked her, she still took some of the blame. She told me we'd hurt him too big, that she'd led him on too long. I told her she was wrong. She didn't lead him on, she loved him the only way she could. She loved him and kept the rest of us safe. We didn't deserve her, not my mom, and not her parents. I hoped she'd be able to work through that. I hated that she didn't see she did nothing wrong.

I promised her I'd spend all our days together making it up to her for my complicity in allowing her to shoulder everything Nathan. She had no business being responsible for him, and that was on all of us. The adults most of all, but I knew my brother was always on the edge and had no control. I should've pushed our mother to make sure he got the mental health care he needed.

Today was one of the days I was doing something for her peace of mind.

Savy wanted to go visit Nathan before we moved away. She wanted to see for herself that he was okay. I supposed a love like the one she cultivated for my brother had an enduring loyalty. Loving him shaped her into the selfless wild beauty that she was today, and for that, I was grateful.

"You ready?" We were parked in front of his facility, sitting quietly side by side and holding hands.

"No." She squeezed my fingers. "I'm nervous."

"Tell me what's making you feel that way." I wanted to know all her emotions, always. No holding back, not after the things we'd endured.

"I'm nervous that he won't look like himself, that he won't sound the same. I'm scared he'll be so medicated he can't function, and he won't even recognize me." She was staring out the window, her eyes searching the big brick building looming beside us.

My dad never wanted to medicate Nathan because he had the same fears as Savy was having now. "Our dad used to say the exact same thing."

"He did?"

"Yeah, he did." It didn't shock me that she wouldn't recall that. She and Nathan were so young when he died. But maybe somewhere, in the back of her mind, she remembered. Maybe her fears were my dad's fears, coming from a repressed memory and haunting her thoughts in the present. "There are only two options here, baby. We go in and visit Nathan, or we don't. The decision is up to you."

She nodded, a resolved look settling across her pretty face. She opened her car door, stepped out, and then reached for my hand as we walked up the front steps. We had to be buzzed inside, then we had to leave all our belongings with the front desk nurse.

Everything smelled clean, but not like a hospital. It was more…fresh. The first floor windows were open, letting in the late summer air. There were bars on them. A reminder of where we were and who was housed here, but the place didn't scream mental hospital.

We passed a game room with a big screen TV. There were some patients hanging out. A few of them were laughing over a ping pong table. With every step we took, I could feel Savy's grip start to relax. This wasn't a hospital where nightmares were made. This was a facility were people went to get help, to get better.

"He's right through there, he's really taken to the library, seems to make him feel the most at home." The nurse pointed through a set of double French doors to a room with floor to ceiling bookshelves.

"How has he been doing?" I knew my mom had been up here a few times to visit, and she'd put me on his medical forms so the doctors and staff could speak to me about him. I also knew that Savy wasn't quite ready to face him yet. She was hiding behind me, her fingers twisting in my shirt.

The nurse smiled. Her hands clasped in front of her. "It was a rough start, as you can imagine. Diagnosis was difficult." That didn't surprise me, none of the doctors he saw as a child could pinpoint a diagnosis either. "He's participating in therapy, and he's engaging with some of the other patients. It seems that we've had some luck with a few different medications."

I could feel Savy stiffen at the mention of medicating Nathan. "How many meds are we talking?"

"Three. But low dose, and all are proven to work well together." The nurse was still smiling, like it was a permanent fixture on her face. "His doctor is in today if you'd like to speak with him. Your mother said you might."

I nodded, reaching behind me and taking Savy's hand. "I'll come find you before we leave, thank you." After the nurse left, I pulled Savy around my body and away from the French doors. "He's participating and engaging, and he likes to hang in the library. That doesn't sound scary, that sounds hopeful." I took her face in my hands, kissing her lips lightly. "Let's go see him, okay?"

She bit at her lower lip, but nodded in agreement. "Yeah, okay."

Nathan was sitting in a leather wing back chair, a large hardback open in his lap. He was leaning to the side, his leg thrown over one arm. He looked relaxed, calm, and comfortable. The doors squeaked as I opened them wider, causing him to glance up from the pages he was focused on. His gaze moved from me to Savy, then back again.

Savy held her hand up in a small wave, and he cocked his head to the side. "Jeremy."

I stepped forward, my hands clasped behind my back, surprised that he wanted to talk to me first. "Hey man, you look—"

"Please leave."

Well. That was more like it. I couldn't say I blamed him. I was in love with the girl of his dreams. But he said please, and I'd take that as a win. I nodded and turned back to Savy. "If you want me to stay, then tell him that. If you're okay speaking to him alone, I'll be right outside those doors. The choice is yours, baby. I'll do whatever you need me to do."

Her attention moved from me to Nathan, who was still sitting in the chair and was once again reading as he waited for me to leave. "I think I'm okay. You can go." She smiled tightly. "Just outside the doors, right?"

I nodded, reaching out to squeeze her hand, not ready to push my luck by kissing her in front of a still becoming stabilized Nathan. "Promise." I looked past her to my brother. "It's really nice to see you Nathan. You look great."

I knew one day I'd be able to speak to my brother again. One day we'd bury the hurt between us. Today not being that day didn't bother me. I cared more about Savy's healing than I did my own, or even Nathan's. She needed this time with him, she needed to see that he was okay, and that she didn't break him.

Chapter Thirty-Three

Savy

I was alone with Nate for the first time since he'd tried to rape me. That was difficult to say, even in my head. I'd been meeting with a therapist weekly. Someone to help me understand and work through my conflicting and warring emotions when it came to what happened between Nate, Jeremy, and me. I stepped forward, my shoes quiet against the hardwood floors. The library looked different from the rest of the facility. Ugh. I hated that word, but hospital didn't seem right either.

Nate sat up straighter, putting both his feet on the ground and closing the book in his lap. I glanced down, noticing it was a biography about Nathaniel Hawthorne. "I'm sorry, Sav." His gaze met mine, and I let out the breath I'd been holding. He was back, the boy I'd grown up with. I could see the emotion in his eyes, the love and the apology. "I hurt you, and I'll never forgive myself."

I sat in the chair opposite his, my hands in my lap. "I forgive you." And I did. That was the first thing I said to my therapist. She asked me why I forgave him, why I thought he deserved my forgiveness. I told her that I'd loved him for too long to stop now. She said that I could love him and not forgive him at the same time. We agreed to disagree. Nate was part of me, woven into every memory I could recall, both good and bad.

"I could see myself scaring you, but I couldn't stop." He shook his head slowly, like he was more or less speaking to himself. "The only person who could pull me back inside myself was lying under me, crying."

I didn't want to relive those moments, I wanted to be in the here and now. "How are you feeling?"

He sighed, leaning back into his chair again. "The pills make me feel a little weird, like everything is softer, but I feel okay." His head turned to the large windows between the bookshelves. "I'll be here for a long time, and that's hard to think about." He sounded sad, which was an emotion he didn't normally give off.

"Would it be okay if I come to visit you again?" I could never leave him in here to heal all alone. The last four weeks were the longest I'd been away from him since the day we met. I wanted to offer to write to him, to email, but I was still wary, still a little afraid that he'd take it as leading him on. There needed to be some boundaries between us, they were long overdue.

He looked back over at me, a small smile on his handsome face. "I'd like that, Sav." His gaze cut to the French doors. "You can bring Jeremy if you want."

I nodded, my heart swelling at the hidden meaning behind his words. "Okay, I'm sure he'd be happy to see you again soon."

Nate was still angry. He hadn't forgiven his brother. But he wanted to see him, even if he refused to admit it out loud. To me, that spoke volumes. Maybe this place, maybe the medications, would work and Nate could learn to be his own salvation. Like I had. I wanted that for him, more than anything. I wanted my best friend to be happy and healthy, to have a life full of love and adventure. "I miss you, Nate."

He leaned forward, slowly reaching for my hand, like he was giving me time to tell him no. I wasn't scared he would hurt me. I could see in his eyes he only wanted to comfort me. "I miss you too, Sav, constantly. I messed up really big this time. I need to be here."

I got to my feet, squeezing his hand before letting go. "I'll see you soon."

"Yeah, see you soon." He smiled at me, then reopened his book.

Epilogue

Jeremy

Eight Months Later

Spring semester was coming to a close, and summer vacation was within reach. Savy and I already decided that we weren't going back home for the break. It was still too fresh being where everything went down. Savy continued seeing her therapist who agreed that there was no reason to put ourselves in a position to feel worse. We were making progress, and in time, going back to our parents' houses would feel okay. I didn't know how long it would take, but when we talked about it, Savy and I agreed, we'd return to our parents' homes when it wouldn't be a big deal anymore.

I'd planned the perfect summer. Savy didn't know it yet, but we were taking a road trip, driving from Boston to the California coast, staying at all kind of places in between. I'd promised her adventures like she'd dreamed about, and I intended to deliver.

"There's my wild one," I shouted. The minute she walked into the party at my apartment, I held out my arms, welcoming her onto my lap. "I hate it when you stay at your place." I kissed her delicious lips while my hands roamed over her bare thighs.

She pulled back smiling. "I get that, but you know how I crave my freedom." She winked, letting me know she was playing.

We'd come a long way, and recently she'd turned a corner in her recovery. Therapy was hard work, but she was committed, strong, resilient, and focused on her health. If anyone knew how important mental well-being was, it was Savannah Nightingale.

"Come with me. I feel the need to have you to myself." I helped her off my lap, ignoring her protests. I took her hand, leading her away from her fan club. Turned out Savy was a social butterfly, and all my friends had taken to her instantly.

She started to giggle when I pulled her down the hall into my bedroom. We lived minutes away from each other, and the nights she stayed at her dorm were absolute torture. I liked falling asleep inside her and waking up to her bright eyes. "Sneaking away from your own party to make out?"

I picked her up, loving the way her long legs wrapped around my waist. "Who said I wanted to make out?" I placed open mouth kisses on her neck. "I plan on fucking you senseless, baby." I fell onto the bed on my back with her settling astride my hips. "I missed you last night."

Her palm rested over my heart, her smile lighting up my dimly lit room. "I missed you too."

"You did?" I rubbed my hands on her thighs, then up to the hem of her shirt, pulling it off and tossing it to the floor. "Well, I have the perfect solution."

She laughed lightly. "Oh yeah? Let me guess. Having my perfectly good dorm room go to waste. My parents would *love* that."

Savy's relationship with her parents was getting better. Her therapist insisted on a few sessions with her mom and dad present, and one where my mom was in attendance. Savy needed to know that no one blamed her, that the adults in her life were truly sorry for the role they played in everything that went down. Or, actually, the lack of the roles which they should've played.

"How about we get rid of your dorm room altogether, I kick out my roommates, and you move in here with me in the fall." I'd been thinking about it a lot, and nothing would make me happier than having her here with me. We were young, but we were in love. We'd survived so much together, and we were working hard on healing. We deserved this.

She narrowed her eyes, her bottom lip between her teeth. "Now why would I want to move in here with you?" She glanced over her shoulder, taking in my room. "You leave food and plates all over the place."

I tickled her, rolling us over until she was laughing and squirming underneath me. "Small price to pay for constant orgasms though, right?"

She squeezed my waist between her thighs, her laughter fading. "I'm not sure. Why don't you remind me what constant orgasms feels like, and then I'll let you know."

I loved every inch of Savannah Nightingale, every shade of her personality. This Savy, the one wild one with the wicked grin, was my favorite. It had nothing to do with sex, and everything to do with watching my girl demand what she wanted.

I dipped down, claiming her mouth with my own. We worked together, shedding our clothes, letting our hands and lips roam. Her back arched as I entered her, burying myself as far as I possibly could and still needing more. I wanted to be consumed by her, completely taken over by her body and soul.

She moved with me, meeting me thrust for thrust, whimpering. I held myself up with one arm, the other at her hip keeping her pinned to the mattress. I loved watching her, lips parted and eyes on mine.

It was arrogant to think I'd saved her last summer. I saw now that she didn't need rescuing. She was the type of person who loved others more than she loved herself. That was her curse and her gift. She would've liberated herself. She'd been halfway there, insisting on going to a different college than Nathan. She was never meant to be caged, and she knew it.

Her nails raked down my back, making me smirk as I fucked her harder. She bit her lip, trying to hold in her cries. I tugged it out by sucking on it. Sweat coating my brow as I tried to give her everything. "No way baby, let me hear you."

She shook her head, hooking her ankles around my hips, keeping me inside her. "There are people down the hall."

I nodded, nipping at her neck. "I know. Aren't roommates the worst? Tell me to get rid of them and I will."

She snorted, pushing on my shoulder, rolling us back over.

She rode me, her hands on my chest for balance. She was a vision, taking the pleasure she demanded with her long blonde hair swaying and her head thrown back. She came hard, a soft groan on her lips as she stilled above me. Her pussy clenched, milking my dick so fiercely I had no other option but to spill inside her.

She was panting on top of me, trying to catch her breath while I stroked her fevered flesh. "Move in with me, baby. Let me love you every night and kiss you every morning."

She sighed, sitting up with her hands on her slim hips and a smile on her swollen lips. "Wasn't the deal constant orgasms before I gave you my answer?"

I flipped her onto her back, pushing her knees to the mattress. "Tell me now and I'll make you come until the sun's up."

"Promises, promises." She laughed as my teeth clamped on her inner thigh. "Okay, okay. I'll move in with you."

I moved up her body, hovering over her beautiful face. "I love you in a way I never knew existed." I brushed the hair back from her face, hoping like hell she saw the truth in my eyes.

Savy was my whole world. We'd been hurt, she worse than me, and my brother had been a mess most of his life. Now, we were healing.

Nathan still had a lot of work to do, even after eight months he understood that he was nowhere near ready to leave his facility. Savy visited him once a month, making the long drive to be there for her best friend. His doctors said her visits were good for him. They gave him something to look forward to. I went with her for support. Nathan still didn't want much to do with me. He no longer made me leave the room when they hung out, so that was progress.

We'd traveled a broken, ugly road that had led us to this moment, to her in my bed agreeing to move in with me.

If I had it all to do over again, I wasn't sure what I'd change. Savy was who she was because of what she'd endured, and what she'd overcome. I was who I was because *seeing* her, loving her, had made me a man worthy of her attention.

Who could know where any of us would be if we'd done even one small thing differently?

Life was funny like that, and made me appreciate even the parts that hurt like hell.

When I realized I had everything I'd ever wanted, I knew all the pain was worth it.

TURN THE PAGE AND TAKE A SNEAK PEEK AT
THE FOREVER WEEKEND

THE FOREVER WEEKEND

Livi

Airplanes were not my most favorite place to be. They smelled bad and were a breeding ground for bacteria. Not to mention that heavy metal boxes had no business being in the air. But I'd calculated the drive to Georgia, and it wasn't worth it for a long weekend. So, I'd let my best friend drag my ass onto the unnatural monstrosity.

"Are you going to tell them?"

I shook my head as I collapsed into the thin blue leather seat. "Nope."

"You need to tell them."

I rolled my eyes, as I stored my purse in its proper place under my feet. "Yes, Kasey, I'm aware that I need to tell my best friends that I'm getting divorced."

"You should have told them when it happened."

I sighed; this was getting exasperating. Kasey had been giving me a hard time about keeping secrets ever since they called us for boarding. I'd never thought I'd be getting divorced. When I said *I do*, I had every intention of *I Doing* forever. It was more embarrassing than I expected, harder to talk about with the people close to me. I could ramble about my personal life to the grocery store bag boy, and I had, but I was finding it near impossible to open up to my friends.

"It's not so easy to talk about. Not to mention I've been a little busy. I was doing all those pesky things like kicking Patrick out, finding a lawyer, and convincing my mom that I did not need to move in with her." I clicked my seat belt into place, tightening it. "By the time I had a moment's peace, this trip was only a few weeks away. Girls' Trip is for drinking and debauchery, not divorce talk."

"Well, you found the time to tell me."

I snorted. "No, I didn't. You just happened to be on the phone with me when I walked in and caught the man I've been married to for the last five years nailing his brand-new secretary."

I side-eyed the guy who'd sneezed relatively close to my shoulder.

"You found out by default." I looked over at one of my favorite people in the world. Kasey and I met in college at a party our freshman year. We bonded over our love of oldies music and ice-cold beer. Right now, her big brown eyes were full of love and support. I knew she was right, but I was in no way, shape, or form about to ruin our yearly girls' trip with my soon-to-be divorce. "Please drop it for now, Kasey. I *need* this weekend, and I need it to be drama free."

My three best friends and I took one trip a year together, *one*. I wasn't about to spend the next three days doing anything other than drinking, dancing, and laughing with my tribe.

"I'm about to take my antianxiety drops so I can make it through this damn flight." I held up the little brown dropper bottle in my hands. "I swear I miss the old days when we were broke college kids and couldn't afford to fly anywhere." I put two drops of the holistic calming meds under my tongue, ignoring Kasey's laughter. She knew I hated to fly, they all knew I hated to fly. But here I was, yet again, on another flight.

Kasey gasped beside me, then started to shake my shoulder. "Livi, look, is that our pilot? I swear I saw that guy at the bar this morning when we were drinking breakfast."

"Stop. It." I narrowed my eyes trying to determine if she was kidding.

"I'm serious." She was smiling though, fighting back laughter, so she had to be joking.

"Serious pain in my ass. Now leave me alone. You aren't funny." I closed my eyes and tried to steady my breathing. Within a few minutes I started to feel a little woozy, like I'd drunk half a bottle of wine. Hmmm this was a nice way to fly. Within another sixty seconds I felt like I'd switched from wine to tequila. These holistic people knew their stuff.

"Livi? Livi."

I opened one eye when I heard my name. "What now? Did you see our flight attendant doing lines in the bathroom?"

"What? No. We landed. We're here."

I opened the other eye, looking past her out the little round window, amazed that we were on the tarmac. "Really? I slept through the whole flight? I'm gonna be pissed if we haven't even taken off yet, Kasey, I swear—"

"We're really here, weirdo. You've been asleep for like three hours." She started digging around in her purse, grabbing her phone and turning it on. "You're terrible company."

I sat up straighter, stretching my arms above my head. "Sorry. Either I was tired or those are some badass holistic meds my yoga instructor gave me." I felt so alive and refreshed, I needed to send her limber ass a thank you note.

We waited until it was our turn to get off the plane, which seemed to take an eternity. When we rounded the corner, following the signs to baggage claim, I stopped short and put my arm out to get Kasey's attention. "Uh, why is there a handsome young man holding a sign with our names on it? Are we being *Punk'd*?" I started looking around, checking for a hidden camera crew or Ashton Kutcher.

"*Punk'd*?"

The sign holder was more than handsome, he was like handsome times infinity. He had this studious-boy-next-door thing going on. Short blond hair and kind green eyes that were darting all around the airport, searching for us apparently.

Kasey snorted. "What is this, two thousand and three? No one gets *Punk'd* anymore." She tilted her head, giving him an appreciative once-over. "Bailey probably hired drivers so we wouldn't have too many cars at the lake house. Let's head to baggage claim, our luggage should be there by now."

Kasey walked off to grab our bags, I didn't follow her; she was stronger than me. She was used to carrying a toddler on her hip all day, she could handle our two suitcases. Instead, I went to talk to tall, blond, and handsome with the sign. I was too intrigued to wait, and he was clearly looking for us.

"Excuse me, um, sir? I'm Livi. Of Livi and Kasey." I pointed to his sign. "As appealing as this all, uh, seems, did someone send you for us? Because neither Kasey nor Livi," I pointed to the sign again, "would have had the foresight to hire a car service."

He dropped said sign down by his side, giving me an easy smile. "Your friend Bailey hired us." He reached out and took the carry-on strap that was resting on my shoulder.

"Us?" I smiled back. I had no choice, his voice had an adorable Southern edge to it, and was making me slightly giddy. Either that or my meds hadn't worn off completely.

"Yes, ma'am." There it was again, that melt-your-panties-off Southern drawl. "Bailey hired two of us for the weekend. We're from Club Concierge." When all he got in response was silence and my mouth hanging open, he chuckled. "Your friend basically hired male butlers for the next three days."

My eyes went wide. "Oh."

Every girls' trip we joked about hiring some hot man-candy to wait on us hand and foot. And every year we never actually went through with it. Bailey liked to spoil her friends, but hot-man butlers? That took the cake. I glanced behind me as Kasey struggled her way over to join us. The buff butler man handed me the sign and went to help her. Well, he certainly seemed good at his job, didn't he?

"Who did *what*? What did I miss while I was wrestling *all* of our luggage?" Kasey blew her chocolate brown bangs out of her face and shot me a dirty look. "Thanks for the help by the way."

My eyes darted to our new friend. He'd gotten on his cell phone, but I whispered all the same. "Bailey hired us hot-man butlers for the weekend."

"Shut. Up."

"I will not." I pursed my lips, gesturing with my head to the cutie with my carry-on. "That's what *Southern charm* over there said. Apparently, she hired two of them." Please God let the other one be as gorgeous and as Southern as the one easily holding all our bags in his muscular arms. Not that Southern men were in short supply where we were from, we lived in Texas, but let me tell you, there is a difference between the South and the Deep South. FYI, the Deep South, was my weakness. That's not really a pun intended type thing, although it could be. You ladies know what I'm talking about.

When butler number one got off his phone, Kasey stuck out her hand in greeting. "I'm Kasey. It's nice to meet you."

He shifted my bag to his other arm so he could shake her hand. "Cole. Nice to meet you." He glanced to me. "Both of you." He gestured in front of him, indicating that we should go ahead. "My buddy is pulling the truck around to pick us up."

If his buddy was even half as adorable as Cole, it was going to be a hell of a weekend.